# SIX-GUN SIEGE

# SIX-GUN SIEGE

by

BOB STEELE

ARCADIA HOUSE

12

To

Jesse and Jane
Conaway

*Printed in the United States of America*

# SIX-GUN SIEGE

# One

*August 17, 1871. Juan El Pardo held the small border town in a deadly grip of steel. He had but to tighten his fingers and Jurado would disappear in a blazing fury of flame and smoke. . . .*

Sheriff Mace Bowman angled through the inch-deep dust of the street toward the land office. Stopping on the boardwalk in the shadows cast by the shabby building, he swept his hat to the back of his head and swabbed dispiritedly at the rivulets of sweat trickling down his face and dropping steadily from the point of his chin. Silently he cursed the scorching sun, the unreasonable heat and the ill-considered decision which had brought him to the small Texas border town some years before.

The dour-faced clerk behind the counter looked up as the sheriff entered, jerking his head in the direction of a door lettered "Private" at the rear of the room. Bowman eyed him with distaste.

"Webb," he said sourly, "if you ever cracked a smile, I'd count the ten years I've spent in Jurado as wasted!"

He skirted the counter; a gangling, awkward-looking man in his early forties. The awkwardness and shambling gait were deceptive, as more than one border tough had discovered a split-second too late to side-step a one-way ride to Boot Hill. Topping six feet, with black hair and searching dark eyes, he had the disjointed appearance of a man who found it hard to push one foot ahead of the other, until the six-gun strapped to his hip was pressed into action.

He pushed open the door of the private office without knocking, kicking it shut behind him with the heel of a dusty boot. The heavy-set man behind the polished desk and the others seated about the room or lounging with shoulders braced against the wall were all known to him.

"Bowman, I've asked you to knock before you come barging in here!"

The lanky sheriff grinned across the desk at the stocky, powerfully-built land speculator. He said indifferently, "Don't rightly recall, Don."

Don Stillman studied the lawman, poorly veiled animosity in his hard, shrewd eyes. A lawyer by profession, an opportunist by nature, Stillman had migrated to Jurado some years before and promptly began carving a private empire from the sun-baked land. Not above using violence when he thought it necessary, as a rule he favored legal trickery and intimidation to accomplish his purpose.

Bowman mentioned, "Denver said you wanted to see me."

"No doubt you've heard that John Navarre is missing," the land speculator said stiffly. "It's the second mysterious disappearance in three days, Sheriff."

He held up a sheet of paper for the sheriff to examine. Across the top, crudely lettered, were the words "Death List," and below nine names had been carefully spelled out, the top two having heavy lines drawn through them.

Stillman said, "This was left in Navarre's bedroom at his ranch."

Bowman moved up to the desk and took the paper from the lawyer's hand. He read off slowly, "Les Cameron, Nick Valdes, Virgil Storey, Ed Krul, Hank Rivers, Ford Wilson, Don Stillman. Scratched out, Ben Gates and John Navarre."

He glanced around the room, his eyes expressionless.

"Well, I see those of you who can still get around under your own power are here," he observed mildly. "This note is about the same as the one we found out on Ben Gates' spread. Another name scratched out, that's all."

Stillman said caustically, "Is that all you have to say, Bowman? I want to know what you intend doing about this!"

The lean sheriff shrugged his shoulders. "Maybe you've got an idea, Don?"

"You could send a posse out."

"Send them where, Don? As far as the river, but not across? As far as El Pardo's hacienda, but no farther? A few miles to the north or east?"

"If El Pardo had nothing to do with the disappearances, he won't object to you hunting for the men who did!"

Bowman laughed, a dry, humorless sound. "Juan El Pardo is holdin' this town as if it was in a big box, Stillman. Every trail to the outside is guarded, every foot of range in between covered by his *vaqueros*. Anyone can ride in who wants to ride in, but no one rides out!"

He slapped the list of names down hard on the desk in front of the land speculator. "When El Pardo says no one will ride out of here until we turn over the hombres on that list to him, he means *no* one!"

Virgil Storey, seated at the side of the desk near Stillman, snapped, "Let's stop beatin' around the bush, Sheriff! We want El Pardo, and we want him now, before he has all of us dancing on air."

Mace Bowman glanced at the rancher. "Why El Pardo? I can think of plenty of others in the border country who wouldn't mind seein' you all do a rope dance."

Storey said irritably, "It's no secret that outlaw would like to see every man in this room strung up, Bowman."

"I reckon he would," the sheriff conceded. "And with mighty good reason, too! But if I was to gun a man for what I think he's done, I'd start with you hombres right here in this room. Might be a real pleasure, gents!"

Storey retorted, "It's a pleasure you'll never have, mister!"

Stillman said maliciously, "Maybe our sheriff is afraid of this Mexican bandit!"

Bowman glanced coolly at the land speculator, and

Stillman squirmed under the hard scorn in his eyes.

"If I was afraid of anyone, it would be a man like El Pardo," he said bluntly. "But if you're tryin' to needle me into goin' after him, gents, you're wastin' your time. Give me proof instead of gab and I'll move against him!"

"You're a friend of his, Sheriff," Stillman pointed out slyly. "You've known him a long time. It's not likely we could find enough proof to put you on his trail."

"Take off the spurs, Stillman!" the gaunt lawman warned curtly, his eyes narrowing. "The jaspers in this room are all beholden to you one way or another, but I don't owe you a thing!"

His eyes moved over the angry faces of the men in the room. "I reckon you'd all like to see El Pardo out of the way, because you're shakin' in your boots over what he's likely to do. You stole his land and his cattle, or tried to, but I hear you're havin' a little trouble takin' over, Stillman."

"I'll take over!" Stillman rasped. "Depend on it, Sheriff! The courts have ruled El Pardo's family never held legal title to the land, and I filed on it. Nothing wrong with that."

"Nothin' you do is wrong as long as Judge Murphy

has anything to say about it," the lawman agreed dryly. "He's about as big a crook as you are, Don!"

The land speculator flushed and said angrily, "You could be stripped of your badge for talking like that!"

Bowman grinned. "That's what Judge Murphy told me, Don. Seems like a crook hates to be called a crook. No pride in his work, I reckon."

"Have your fun!" Stillman snapped. He nodded his head in a brief signal, and Virgil Storey left his chair and walked to the rear door of the room, swinging it wide. A stranger stood in the alley beyond the opened door. He was almost as tall as Mace Bowman, but younger, with light, nearly white hair and hard, cold eyes. The lawman looked at him, thinking: *Gunman!*

Stillman motioned for the newcomer to enter.

"Dave, this is Mace Bowman, our sheriff," he said as the man reached the desk. "Mace, this gent is Dave Thompson. He'll be our new town marshal."

"Since when?" Bowman asked, ignoring the outstretched hand of the gunman.

"We've been thinking that you have plenty to handle out in the county without being saddled with the problems of the town," the land speculator said smugly. "As head of the Citizens' Committee, I have the authority to make the appointments I feel necessary for the welfare of Jurado."

"Why not?" Bowman asked coolly. "You appointed the Citizens' Committee! What's Thompson's job, Still-man? To gun Juan El Pardo down?"

"His job will be to keep the peace in Jurado," the land office man countered. "Of course, if El Pardo insists upon making trouble, he must be prepared to accept the consequences."

Anger thinned Bowman's lips.

"See to it that your bounty hunter does his dirty work in Jurado," he warned. "Outside the town, he'll be just another hired gun to me."

He pushed his hat to the back of his head and wiped the sweat from his forehead with the sleeve of his shirt. Thompson, calmly appraising the lawman, no-ticed that he performed the ritual with his left hand and arm.

Bowman said easily, with deadly calm, "Thompson, I'll stand you under a hangin' tree if you shoot El Pardo without cause!"

Virgil Storey grumbled, "That's a mighty poor at-titude, Mace! We figured you'd be mighty glad to have Thompson's help."

"The only gunslicks I've worked with are up on Boot Hill!" Bowman said shortly. Wheeling abruptly, he walked from the room.

Dave Thompson rubbed the stubble on the side of his jaw thoughtfully. "Sooner or later me and that sheriff are likely to tangle, gents."

Stillman said sharply, "Stay away from Bowman! You'll be no good to us dead."

The gunman laughed. "You must be funnin', Mr. Stillman! Why, I could ram my gun down that scarecrow's throat before he made up his mind to draw!"

The lawyer glanced knowingly at Virgil Storey. He murmured, "Let's see how you handle your gun, Dave."

Thompson's hand swept with blurring speed, and his six-gun seemed to jump into his hand. Wtih a satisfied grin he twirled it by the trigger guard, then slid it back into his holster. "Good enough."

Ed Krul spoke from his position near the window. "Mighty pretty, Thompson! Thing is, if Mace Bowman had been bucking you just then, you'd be stretched out on Don's nice new carpet!"

Dave Thompson turned toward the speaker, his eyes cold. "Maybe you'd like to try your hand, mister?"

Krul sputtered, and Stillman said roughly, "That's enough, Thompson! Save your talents for the job we brought you here for."

He added placatingly, "Ed was only trying to be helpful, Dave. Maybe you've never heard of Mace Bowman, but he's mighty well known along the border. Take my word for it; you can't beat him in an open gunfight."

Thompson shrugged, but his lips were tight. "Maybe I'll look into the matter later on. When do I start this job you mentioned?"

Stillman said promptly, "The sooner the better!"

Nodding, the gunman turned away. He came to a stop at the door leading to the alley and spoke over his shoulder. "You've got five hundred dollars on El Pardo's head. Any price on Bowman's?"

"You've been told your job," the lawyer said gruffly.

Thompson grinned. "Just thought I'd ask!"

The gunman closed the door behind him, and Ed Krul moved to the desk.

"Thompson's not a man easy to cotton to," he said sourly. "He's likely to cause more trouble than El Pardo and Bowman together."

Virgil Storey agreed. "He's bad medicine, Don."

"He's a hired gun, nothing more," Stillman assured them, waving his hand deprecatingly. "When he's finished here, we'll send him on his way."

Storey murmured, "I hope it's as simple as that."

Dave Thompson walked down the narrow alley to the dusty, heat-choked street. Pacing slowly along the boardwalk, he painstakingly studied the physical aspects of the small border town. A methodical man, leaving nothing to chance, he circled the streets twice before he was satisfied, finally turning in at the sheriff's office. Mace Bowman was there with Denver Rogers, one of his deputies. The gunman found a chair near the open door and dropped into it, thoughtfully fingering the gleaming new badge fastened to the front of his shirt.

"Figured you'd brief me on the town," he remarked at last, looking up at Bowman. "Appears like Don Stillman has his brand on about everything worth-while around here."

"The land office, the bank, two saloons, a hardware store and the livery stable," Bowman told him coolly.

Thompson whistled softly. "Understand he owns a ranch or two."

"Nine," Bowman returned curtly. "Those gents who hired you to gun El Pardo call themselves ranchers and run the spreads, but Stillman is the gent holding the reins."

The sheriff's blunt words grated on the gunman's

nerves, but he held his temper. "You've got it all wrong, Bowman. It's not my intention to brace El Pardo unless he steps out of line."

Bowman said nothing, but his searching gaze never left the gunman's face.

"I counted six hombres in the land office, besides Stillman," Thompson observed. "Who are the others?"

Bowman pushed his hat to the back of his head and dabbed at his face with a soiled bandana. Again the gunman noted that he used his left hand, his right never being far from the black-handled six-gun strapped to his hip.

"There's been a couple of disappearances lately," Bowman said finally. "Ben Gates turned up missing about three days ago, and John Navarre disappeared from his spread last night. Both of those gents just happened to be runnin' cattle on range Stillman took over from the Mexicans."

"What's the connection?" the gunman asked.

"Didn't Stillman fill you in on what's goin' on around here?"

"He mentioned a jasper by the name of El Pardo who seems to be ridin' a rough trail and stirrin' up a lot of dust along the border. Wanted someone to sort of tame him down a mite."

Mace Bowman left his chair behind the desk and moved to the open door, searching for a cooling breeze and finding none. The street was all but deserted, except for an occasional darting lizard and Manuel Hernandez, the blind *vaquero* who seldom left his chair in front of the Maverick.

He said over his shoulder, "Maybe Stillman forgot to tell you why El Pardo is ridin' tall in the saddle."

"Can't see where it makes any difference," Thompson returned. "A gent travels on the right side of the trail or he don't. It's as simple as that."

Bowman turned away from the door.

"Maybe it's that way," he agreed. "When I saw you with that badge pinned on your shirt, it crossed my mind you might feel more at home on the other side of the trail."

The gunman's face darkened. "What's that supposed to mean?"

The lawman said shortly, "Take it any way you want!"

Thompson studied the sheriff for several moments, his eyes bleak with the anger seething within him. Not without courage, he still wanted no part of a showdown brought about by Mace Bowman's deliberate prodding. Knowing he would have to brace the lawman sooner or later, he intended it to be in his own time and on his own terms.

He said smoothly, "You were talkin' about El Pardo and Stillman's holdings, Sheriff."

Bowman circled the corner of the desk and slumped into his chair. He knew now that the cold-eyed gunman could not be goaded into making a move he had not first carefully planned. Maybe that was the reason he'd stayed alive so long, the lawman thought idly.

"Don Stillman came to Jurado about six years ago," he told Thompson. "Claimed to have been a lawyer in some big city back east. Anson Murphy rode in a month or two later, and Stillman somehow managed to have him appointed a judge. No one seems to know much about either of them before the day they suddenly appeared in town.

"Stillman took to studyin' the Spanish grants of the big haciendas around Jurado, lookin' for legal flaws. One by one he took them into Murphy's court, and the judge declared them void because of some technicality. All Stillman had to do was file a claim and move in."

Thompson was impressed. "As simple as that?"

"Not at first," Bowman returned. "The owners tried to fight him through Murphy's court, but that was worse than a waste of time. Some of them fought back with guns and violence, even barricadin' themselves on their spreads, but that didn't work out, either. The time they wasted tryin' to fight Stillman legally gave him enough time to build up a mighty strong bunch of toughs.

"A few floggin's, a couple of bad accidents, a lynchin' or two, and the Mexicans didn't have the stomach to fight him any longer. Most of them just picked up their stuff and moved below the line, leavin' their spreads for Stillman and his pards."

"A mighty slick hombre," the gunman said admiringly. "I take it you couldn't pin anything on him?"

"Not because I didn't try!" Bowman retorted. "But Stillman covered his tracks mighty well, with the help of Murphy and his crooked pards. He had things pretty much his own way until he tried to take over Felipe El Pardo's hacienda."

The gunman murmured, "This Felipe, is he the hombre raisin' all the cain around here?"

Bowman shook his head. "Felipe was Juan El Pardo's father. The old man ran into a fatal accident about the time Stillman decided to take over his hacienda. Seems his foot got snagged in his stirrup and his cayuse dragged him to death."

Denver Rogers spoke for the first time. "Accident, my eye! The whole shebang was rigged to get rid of

Felipe, and that's just what it did."

Bowman nodded his agreement. "We couldn't prove a thing against Stillman, but this time I figure he's bit off more than he can chew."

"This young El Pardo," Thompson asked, "salty, is he?"

"Salty enough to keep Stillman from movin' in on him for almost a month," Rogers told him. "And tough enough to seal this town off from the rest of Texas for five days runnin'."

Thompson looked doubtful. "I didn't see any guards on the main trail when I rode in."

Rogers grinned. "Try ridin' out again, mister!"

Thompson shrugged. "I'm happy here." And as an afterthought, "Why didn't Stillman send in his toughs and clean El Pardo out like he did the others?"

"Juan has a passel of *vaqueros* sidin' him now," Bowman said, "and more ridin' in every day. Put them behind a walled hacienda, and you'd need a small army to get them out."

"You haven't corraled him, Sheriff," the gunman mused. "How is that?"

"What do I charge him with?" Bowman demanded gruffly. "Scarin' Stillman half to death? I know of no warrant out for El Pardo."

"Maybe we can find a way to remedy that," the gunman remarked, climbing to his feet. "Reckon I'll take another turn around town."

Before he reached the doorway, Bowman called, "Thompson!" and the gunman turned.

"There's two kinds of law along the border," the tall sheriff said evenly: "the kind written in a book and the kind I'm carryin' on my hip. I use the one best suited to the occasion."

He patted his holstered gun significantly.

"Juan El Pardo is a friend of mine," he said flatly. "And the law says he's innocent until he's proven guilty. Keep that in mind when you get a hankerin' to earn Stillman's five hundred dollars."

Thompson was annoyed, and it showed clearly in the cold stare he turned on the sheriff. He nodded. "I'll remember, Sheriff."

He left the office and walked aimlessly along the boardwalk until he came to the Maverick, the largest of the four saloons in Jurado and one of the two owned by Don Stillman. He felt no particular need of a drink, but experience had taught him that a saloon in a strange town was the easiest and quickest place to gather information.

He stepped through the swinging doors under a

crudely lettered sign reading: "OPEN TWENTY-FOUR HOURS A DAY," and found himself in a dimly lighted room all of a hundred feet in length. A highly polished bar ran almost the entire length of one wall, with hundreds of bottles balanced on shelves in front of and between the huge mirrors. The second floor consisted of a balcony on three sides of the room, a large number of doors opening out on it, and a long stairway near the rear of the building giving access to the main floor.

The big saloon was almost deserted at that hour. A few weary-eyed card players at a table near the bar were engaged in a half-hearted game of poker, and an early drunk slept fitfully in a far corner. A flamboyantly dressed girl leaned on the far end of the bar, apparently engaged in deep conversation with the mustached bartender, and others left their rooms on the balcony from time to time, peering over the balustrade to see if the number of customers warranted the trip downstairs.

The gunman moved to the center of the bar, casually inspecting the big room as he waited for the bartender to bring a bottle and glass. At the end of the bar, the girl who had been talking to the barkeep glanced his way and decided he looked prosperous enough to stand the price of a drink or two. Thompson watched with interest as she walked toward him.

"I'm Maxine," she announced, stopping at his side. "You're Dan Thompson, the new marshal."

The gunman signaled for another glass and poured a second drink as he openly appraised the girl. Twenty or twenty-one, he judged, dark-haired and softly pretty, not yet showing the brutal effects of smoke-filled barrooms, frontier men and forty-rod whiskey. After a moment, the girl asked coyly, "Do I pass?"

Thompson grinned and met her eyes, lifting his glass in a mock salute. "Here's to a long and happy friendship!"

"You're not a bad-looking gent when you smile," the girl said. "What brings you to this God-forsaken country?"

Thompson removed his hat and tossed it on the bar. "Money. Is there anything else?"

Maxine laughed. "If there is, I haven't found it yet!"

She reached up and touched the badge pinned to the front of his shirt. "You won't get rich wearing that."

"Depends a lot on how a man uses it," Thompson returned.

The girl glanced up at him. "Maybe you've picked the wrong way."

Thompson poured himself another drink. "How so?"

"I'm only guessing that you think the badge will help you bring Juan El Pardo in," she replied, "But don't count Stillman's five hundred dollars before you have it in your pocket, Mister Marshal!"

"News travels mighty fast around here," the gunman said gruffly, scowling. "Why do you think I'm after El Pardo?"

"Jurado knew you were riding in, and why, almost as soon as Stillman sent for you," the girl told him. "That's the way of the town."

The gunman asked casually, "This Mexican badman ever come to Jurado?"

"Sometimes, but more often it's his *vaqueros* who ride in for a few drinks or to pick up supplies for the hacienda."

"Any of them come in here?"

Maxine shrugged her shoulders. "Why not? The whiskey here is no worse than in the other saloons."

Thompson abruptly changed the subject. "Like to go ridin' in the mornin'?"

Maxine studied the gunman, strangely fascinated by the hard ruthlessness so thinly veiled by his easy manner and quick smile. "All right. But make it early, before the sun gets too hot."

A small, slender man dressed in the range clothing of a *vaquero* came through the batwings and found a place at the long bar. Maxine nodded her head in his direction.

"You asked about El Pardo's *vaqueros*," she said in a low voice. "The man who just walked in rides with him. Rafael Benavides. He's a relative of Juan's, a cousin or something."

Thompson reached over and picked up his hat, replacing it carefully on his head. He continued his idle conversation with the girl as she covertly studied the Mexican over her shoulder.

"About Mace Bowman," he remarked, "everyone seems to think he's a grizzly bear in a gunfight."

"Walk a big circle around him, Dave," she said soberly. "He doesn't look like much, but he's poison with that six-gun of his."

Thompson finished his careful appraisal of the Mexican and apparently was satisfied with what he saw. He picked up his glass and bottle and started down the bar, calling over his shoulder, "I'll be seein' you first thing in the mornin'."

He set his glass on the bar beside the dark-skinned *vaquero* and poured a drink. Still holding the bottle in his hand, he turned to Benavides, a wide grin on his lips. But his words, spoken so quietly only the Mexican could hear them, were far from friendly.

"You son of a pig, You dog! You've got plenty of sand, drinkin' whiskey in a white man's saloon!"

Still smiling broadly, he waved the bottle as if offering the *vaquero* a drink. "Get out, pig! Get out of Jurado and stay out!"

The Mexican, momentarily stunned by the viciousness of the unprovoked attack, suddenly spun away from the bar, eyes blazing. His right hand streaked for the holster at his hip, but the gun it encased was more of an ornament than a lethal weapon, and he was far too slow for the hard-eyed, cruelly smiling gunman. The long barrel of the weapon was still touching leather when Thompson's bullet hammered into his chest, driving him in a spinning half-circle back against the bar.

Benavides dropped his gun and clutched at the bar with both hands in a futile effort to keep on his feet. His strength gone, his eyes blurring with pain, his knees buckled and he slid slowly down the polished boards on the bar to a kneeling position. He was still in that position, head inclined against the bar as if in solemn prayer, when the gunman thumbed back the hammer of his gun and slowly lowered the muzzle for another shot at almost point-blank range.

A shot roared out from near the door, and Thompson grunted in pain as the six-gun spun from numbed fingers. Mace Bowman stood near the bat-wings, smoking gun in hand; then he and Denver Rogers were running toward the fallen man. Rafael Benavides was still alive, but his eyes were closed and he breathed with a hard, rasping sound. Rogers motioned to some bystanders, and the stricken Mexican was quickly carried from the saloon.

Bowman turned to the gunman, who still cradled his stinging fingers against his chest. He said in a colorless voice, "Tell me about this, Thompson."

The gunman remained silent, his eyes fastened on Bowman's face, until he picked up his gun, reloaded it and dropped it back into its holster. He said finally, thinly veiled anger in his voice, "You had no cause to butt in here, Sheriff."

"Why did you pull a gun on Benavides?"

"Someone told me this jasper was a relative of El Pardo's," Thompson replied tightly. "Figured if I bought him a drink and palavered a little, he might set me straight about a few things."

Bowman looked over the gunman's shoulder and met the eyes of the dance hall girl. Maxine dropped her eyes and turned away. Bowman said sharply, "You can't get information from a dead man!"

"The Mexican went for his iron first," Thompson retorted. "Any of these hombres will tell you that."

"I reckon you could afford to let a man like Benavides make the first grab," Bowman conceded sourly. "Rafael most likely never drew a gun for anything more deadly than killin' a rattlesnake or a prairie dog."

The gunman shrugged. "I don't generally ask a man's pedigree when he's figurin' on plantin' a bullet under my hide."

"You were about to shoot him again when I walked in. He didn't have a gun on you then."

"Even when a snake is chopped in pieces, he can still sink his fangs in you!"

Bowman turned to the bartender. "Mike?"

Mike Collins waved his hands in a futile gesture. "Wasn't close enough to hear anything, Mace, but to give the devil his due, I reckon the marshal is tellin' the straight of it. Rafael went for his gun first, but Thompson was a heck of a lot faster."

"Seems like he was," Bowman agreed dryly.

Thompson asked mockingly, "Any more questions, Sheriff?"

"Not from me, but El Pardo might have a few,"

Bowman replied grimly. "He won't take kindly to this, Thompson."

The gunman touched the brim of his hat with his fingers and left the saloon, a grin still on his lips. Bowman turned to the bar and poured himself a drink as Mike Collins leaned his elbows on the bar, his eyes puzzled.

"Can't understand it, Mace," he remarked. "Rafael never was a gent to cause any trouble."

"I savvy it," Bowman said thoughtfully. "I'm wonderin' if El Pardo will!"

## *Two*

The stagecoach came to a squealing stop, and Kerby, glancing through the open window at his side, saw the weather-faded sign over the station declaring the town to be Jurado. The only passenger on the incoming stage, he retrieved his gear from the floor at his feet and stepped down into the heavy dust of the street. Narrowing his eyes against the sudden brilliance of the late afternoon sun, he walked slowly toward the veranda of the Border Hotel.

A tall man, wide-shouldered and a little stooped, Jim Kerby moved with the inherent grace and ease of his Shoshone mother as he crossed the almost deserted street. With piercing black eyes and a somber, craggy face, Kerby looked the part of a rough man; hard to understand, dangerous to cross.

He paused near the veranda steps, glancing down

the single street of the small town. It was ten years almost to the day since he had last seen Jurado, and then from this very spot as he had waited impatiently for the outgoing stage to take him away. He saw little change in the sleepy border town. The dreary buildings were a little more weather-worn, a little less solid; the few people whose needs forced them to brave the scorching heat were a little more round-shouldered, a little more resigned.

"Kerby!"

The tall man wheeled, loosening his grip on the saddlebags and dropping without conscious thought into a wary half-crouch. Slowly he straightened, a wry grin on his lips, remembering the six-gun securely strapped within one of the bags. His eyes slitted against the torturing glare of the sun, seeking a clue to the identity of the vague figure standing in the shadows of the hotel. At last the speaker stepped away from the wall into the sunlight, and the tautness seeped from Kerby's nerves.

"Thompson!" he said harshly. Then he saw the glint of sunlight on metal near the center of the gunman's shirt, and his lip curled.

He said scornfully, "A marshal! Who would pin a badge on a dry-gulchin' killer like you?"

He could see the angry blood staining the man's cheeks as he came to a stop ten feet away.

"You're a great hombre to talk about killin'!" Dave Thompson declared, his eyes dropping to Kerby's barren hip. "I paid the goin' rate for the mistake I made, but you were luckier. You did your killin' behind a badge, just like the one I'm wearin', and they couldn't touch you!"

The tall man said curtly, "You called my name. Have your say and move aside."

Thompson looked at the somber figure standing before him, dislike heavy in his eyes. "How long you plan on stayin' in Jurado?"

Kerby considered for a moment, watching the other.

"A day, a year, a lifetime," he said at last. "What difference does it make in the end?"

The gunman shifted his feet restlessly. "Maybe Jurado ain't the way you remembered it, Kerby. Folks change; things change. Maybe the next town would be more to your likin'."

The stranger asked softly, "Is that an order, Marshal?"

"A thought, nothing more," Thompson replied coolly. "But this is my town, all of it. Keep it in mind."

Kerby bent and picked up his saddlebags. As he

moved away he mentally cursed the strange fate which had brought the two men together in Jurado. He remembered the gunman-turned-marshal only too well. Seven years before, as a deputy sheriff in Laramie, Kerby had tracked down and arrested Thompson for the bushwacking robbery and murder of an old cattleman. Working carefully, he had prepared what he believed to be an air-tight case against the gunman.

Before the day set for the trial, Kerby was forced to stand idly by as Thompson's companions persuaded the witnesses, sometimes with fear, sometimes with stolen money, to conveniently disappear or alter their stories. At the trial Thompson pleaded guilty to manslaughter and so escaped the hangman's rope. The stern-faced judge had sentenced him to a ten-year term in the territorial prison, but Thompson had served little more than two years before he was given his freedom by a lenient parole commission.

Kerby pushed through the door of the Border Hotel, started to salute when he recognized old Asa Duggan behind the desk, then dropped his hand to his side when he saw the cold, unfriendly expression on the clerk's face.

He said quietly, "I'd like a room, and a little water to wash away the trail dust, Asa."

Duggan spun the ledger around and tossed a pencil in front of him. "Five dollars a day, in advance."

Kerby scrawled his name in the ledger. He asked evenly, "Is that a special rate for me, Asa?"

"Take it or leave it!" the old man snapped. "We don't need your kind around here."

Kerby tossed two silver dollars on the desk. "I'll have a key."

Duggan started a retort but thought better of it when he saw Kerby's cold eyes watching him. He dropped a key in front of the ex-lawman.

"Second floor, third door on the right," he said gruffly. "The marshal will hear about this!"

Kerby unpacked his saddlebags in the dingy room, taking a folded newspaper out last. He stretched out wearily on the bed and opened the paper, a two-month-old edition of the *Abilene Dispatch.* For the hundredth time he read the bitterly accusing headlines:

"GUN-HAPPY MARSHAL KILLS BOY!"

And below it, in fine print, was an even more damning text:

"Young Bill Janus died last night, a bullet in his heart. Only a youngster, little more than sixteen, he was shot and killed by Marshal Jim 'Shoot-First-And-Ask-Questions-Later' Kerby, who claimed he caught the boy in the act of rifling the safe in the Wells Fargo office.

"This is not the first time Marshal Kerby has found it convenient to use a quick gun, but Billy is by far his youngest victim to date. On several occasions during the six months Kerby has served as marshal of Abilene, this newspaper and various city officials have received complaints—"

Kerby tossed the paper to the floor, passing his hand wearily across his eyes. There was more to the article, much more, and all of it hostile to the ex-marshal. It re-hashed other shootings in which he had taken part, coloring the facts and castigating him unmercifully.

And for the hundredth time Kerby silently cursed the twist of fate which had sent his bullet, intended for the boy's gun hand, crashing into his chest. Billy Janus had dived for the shelter of the open safe door just as Kerby triggered his weapon, and the bullet intended to disarm the boy had instead ended his life.

At the time of the incident, Kerby had bitterly resented what he felt was a deliberate omission by the *Dispatch* of many of the facts in the unfortunate shooting, and this resentment had lead him to resign his post and leave Abilene. The writer of the article had

failed to point out that young Janus had fired four
shots at the marshal, the final shot cutting a deep gash
in his left shoulder; or that Kerby had first fired two
warning shots into the air, shooting at the boy's gun
hand only after he himself had been wounded. Neither
was there any mention of the fact that the two older
brothers of Billy Janus, both notorious gunmen and
outlaws, also had been at the scene of the attempted
robbery, deserting the boy and making good their escape seconds before the gun battle began.

A knock sounded on the door, and Kerby twisted
over on his side, calling, "It's open!"

The gruff, unfriendly room clerk poked his head into
the room. "Someone in the lobby to see you."

Kerby asked, "Who is it?" but the sound of the door
slamming was his only reply.

He strapped on his gun and walked from the room.
Pausing at the head of the stairs, he could see the room
clerk's desk and a part of the lobby. His heart lifted
as he recognized the trim figure of the pretty girl standing near the desk, impatiently twisting a white handker-
chief between her fingers. Kerby thought of his last
meeting with Mary Pearson, and a little of the joy left
him at the memory of the bitterness with which they had
parted.

At the time, he had been sure he loved the vivacious girl and he had thought that she loved him in return. But Kerby wanted a lawman's badge, and Mary was adamant in her refusal to marry him if he persisted in his ambition.

"I'd die a little each time you walked away from me," Mary had said, tears glistening in her eyes, "not knowing if I'd ever see you alive again. I couldn't take that, Jim. Find another job and I'll marry you today."

On that day almost ten years before, Kerby, hurt and bitter because of what he thought was lack of confidence in him, had turned and walked away. Now, as he approached the girl, his heart beat a little faster and he knew he had never completely forgotten all the girl had once meant to him.

He took her hand. "Mary!"

The girl glanced about the lobby; then raised herself to her toes and kissed him lightly on the lips.

"That's so you'll know I don't believe everything I read in the papers," she whispered, her cheeks suddenly flushed.

The ex-marshal took her arm, and together they walked to a leather-covered sofa in a corner of the room. Seated beside her, he raised her left hand to the light and found it free of rings.

"Ten years is a long time, Mary," he said soberly. "How is it you passed by all the young buckaroos who used to camp on your Dad's front porch?"

The girl smiled a little wistfully. "Maybe it's because I couldn't forget a tall black-haired boy with a yearning to be a lawman!"

She turned, facing him. "Tell me about it, Jim. Abilene, I mean. Maybe talking will help."

Reluctantly, Kerby outlined the story the *Abilene Dispatch* had failed to print.

"It's mostly a matter of dimes and dollars," he concluded. "The merchants and saloon keepers never wanted a tough marshal or a quiet town."

He grinned ruefully. "You've been listenin' to my troubles, Mary, but it seems you folks here in Jurado have a few of your own. They tell me young Juan El Pardo is stirrin' up a lot of dust along the border."

"With good reason," the girl replied. She gave him a brief account of the happenings in the town since the arrival of Don Stillman.

"I remember Juan," Kerby said when she had finished. "Never figured him for a gent likely to kick over the traces."

Dave Thompson came through the door, and Kerby

rose to his feet, extending a hand to the girl. He said in a low voice, "I'll see you tonight."

Mary smiled up at him and walked past the oncoming gunman, her eyes averted. Thompson watched the girl pass through the doorway, his eyes calculating. Finally he turned back to Kerby, apparently about to make a flippant remark, but the ex-marshal held up his hand warningly.

"Don't say it, Thompson!" he said coldly. "Don't even mention her name."

Thompson growled, "You're a mighty proddy gent, friend."

Kerby said nothing.

"Who sent for you?" Thompson asked suddenly.

Kerby said evenly, "Even if I knew what you were talkin' about, I'd still consider it none of your business."

"You keep runnin' off at the mouth that way and someone's likely to lose it for you, permanent."

"You?"

"Maybe."

"You'll have to be a mite better than you were seven years ago, Marshal."

"I reckon I am."

Kerby laughed scornfully. "Maybe you are, Thompson, but you'll never pull that gun of yours until you're certain. I know your breed like I know the palm of my hand."

"You come lookin' for trouble?"

"Not lookin' for it, but not side-steppin' it, either!"

Pushy, like Bowman, Thompson thought idly. Aloud he said, "All right, Kerby. But there's things happenin' in Jurado, things that don't concern you. Might be best if you didn't take sides."

Kerby spun on his heel and left the hotel.

On the street he paused for a moment, undecided, then headed in the direction of the Maverick.

"Kid killer!"

The words, sharp and clear, came from behind him. Kerby stepped from the broadwalk, turned slowly and planted his feet firmly in the dust of the street. His eyes picked out the figure of a man lounging in the shade of Temper's Gun Shop.

"Anderson!" he said tightly, recognizing the man instantly even after ten years. "You always did have a big mouth, Cliff, and no sand to back it up."

Virgil Storey's range foreman took his shoulder from the wall and moved out into the sunlight. His face was flushed, and Kerby guessed his sudden courage had come from an all-night bout with a whiskey bottle.

"Don't need much sand to brace a kid," Anderson taunted, his voice thick.

Kerby shifted his feet in the dust of the street, moving his shoulders to ease the tension. "You're drunk, mister. Think about this a mite."

"I read the papers, Kerby. We don't think any more of you here than they did in Abilene."

Farther along the street, Kerby saw Mary Pearson come out of her millinery shop, and a strange, sudden anger swept over him. His eyes slid back to the half-drunken man in front of him.

He said coldly, "You're wearin' a gun, Cliff. Use it or step aside!"

Anderson backed off a step. He said loudly, "I'm no gunman, Kerby. I've no intention of drawin' against you!"

The ex-lawman said evenly, "I said you're all mouth, Cliff."

"But I'm alive, and you may not be much longer! I hear tell that kid had a couple of brothers who're mighty handy with a gun."

The ex-marshal was quiet for a moment, his somber eyes studying the red-faced range boss. Then he laughed contemptuously, and the harsh sound of it brought a deeper flush to the features of Cliff Anderson. Kerby turned away; then, knowing the caliber of his man, he spun around in a complete turn and stabbed for his gun.

Anderson's weapon was out and leveling, but the ex-lawman's shot was first by half a breath, driving the range foreman back against the wall of the gun shop. The six-gun he was holding dropped from fingers suddenly without feeling, and the would-be gunman collapsed on the boardwalk, holding his shattered arm and moaning with pain.

Kerby holstered his gun and came up, sweeping the fallen gun into the street with his boot. Thin-lipped, he stood looking down at the whimpering man.

"Count yourself lucky, friend," he said curtly. "You might have been on your way to Boot Hill right now."

He wheeled away as rough hands picked up the wounded man and hustled him off the street. A moment later he stepped through the swinging doors of the Maverick, standing motionless just inside until his eyes adjusted themselves to the dimness of the big room.

"Howdy, Jim!"

Kerby picked out the speaker where he stood at the near end of the bar. He moved up, signaling the bartender with a nod of his head.

He said nonchalantly, "Hello, Mace."

"It's been a long time," Bowman remarked, his shrewd eyes appraising the face of the ex-marshal. "You haven't changed much, Jim. Only a little older, like the rest of us."

Kerby nodded but said nothing. He took the bottle Mike Collins set before him and poured out a stiff drink.

Bowman, said, "I watched that little fracas you had with Anderson. No one would have blamed you for puttin' that bullet in his heart instead of his arm."

Kerby tossed off the drink, poured another.

"Cliff was drunk," he said without emotion. "I don't reckon he'd have braced me, sober."

"A bullet from a drunk's gun kills you just as dead as any other," Bowman returned mildly. "Anderson runs with a pack of rats; now he's actin' like one. Don't turn your back on him."

Kerby shrugged, and Bowman said, "What brings you to Jurado?"

Kerby spun the empty glass between his fingers. The bartender stood nearby, trying to conceal his interest in the conversation of the two men by methodically swabbing at the surface of the bar.

"Thompson asked me that," the ex-marshal countered. "Seems like everyone is mighty interested in me all of a sudden!"

"Not in you, Jim," Bowman said evenly, "but in knowing on which side of the fence you'll light."

Kerby said irritably, watching the bartender out of the corner of his eyes, "I don't know anything about fences, Mace. I'm not takin' sides, one way or the other."

"I could use a good deputy," Bowman said tentatively.

"No," Kerby said flatly. "I'm all through with that, Mace. Ten years of totin' a badge and gettin' spit on is enough for any man."

"It's the way you look at it, I reckon." The lanky sheriff shrugged. "Enforcin' the law never was easy, Jim. Thing is, a man learns early to spit just a little harder than the other gent. Most times he gets the idea."

"And if he doesn't, you prod him with a six-gun or tuck a bullet under his hide," Kerby retorted. "Either way, you're dirt to most folks."

"Only to the ones who don't matter," Bowman insisted. "The ones tryin' to run a business or raise a family know what they owe to the man wearin' a badge."

Kerby was staring over the lawman's shoulder, and Bowman turned, following his gaze. Maxine, the dance hall girl, was standing at the far end of the bar, in deep conversation with Dave Thompson. At that moment the girl lifted her eyes and saw Kerby standing beside the sheriff. Even at that distance Bowman could see the shocked expression on her face. Then she turned swiftly, her back to the two men.

Bowman asked idly, "Know her, Jim?"

Something resembling pain flitted across the ex-marshal's face, but vanished so quickly Bowman could not be certain he had seen it.

"No," Kerby said at last, but his voice lacked conviction. "She looks like someone I knew a long time ago. Just a mistake."

Still puzzling over the incident, Bowman finished his drink and left the saloon. When Kerby looked again, he saw that Thompson had disappeared and the girl was just mounting the stairs to the second floor.

The door of the room opened instantly at his knock, and Maxine looked up at him, her face pale.

The door opened wider, and Kerby stepped into the room. He saw the gaudy costumes on their hangers, the bottles and boxes on the vanity, and his lips tightened.

He said, trying to keep his voice even, "Why?"

Maxine shrugged her shoulders. "A girl has to make a living, Jim."

As he studied the girl in silence, Kerby's thoughts drifted back four years. She was not yet seventeen when he first met her in Cheyenne, Kerby had thought she was everything he wanted in a woman. The daughter of a struggling rancher on the outskirts of town, she was seemingly untouched by the hard frontier life.

A month later, on her seventeenth birthday, Kerby and Maxine stood in front of a traveling padre and listened to the solemn words of the marriage ceremony. To Kerby the first few months of the union produced a happiness far beyond anything he had ever dreamed or hoped for, and he had every reason to believe his beautiful young wife shared his feelings.

His job as a deputy sheriff took him away from home often in the months following his marriage. At first his frequent absences seemed to make little difference, but little by little he was aware of a change in his young bride, and at last bits of gossip began reaching his ears.

Angrily he tried to track the malicious stories to their source, but with little success.

They had been married less than a year when he returned from a ten-day trip to southern Montana to find his wife gone and a pink sheet of paper propped up on the kitchen table. Its message was brief and cruel:

*"Jim—There's nothing between us any more. Thanks for everything."* And it was signed, *"Maxine."*

He repeated in a dead voice, "Why?"

Maxine turned away from him, moved to a window and looked down into the heat-simmering street.

"Jim," she said, choosing her words carefully, "there could never really be anything between us. Maybe at first it was all right; we were young and we thought we loved each other. But deep inside I was never your kind of girl and never could be. I wanted gayety and excitement, and when you weren't there to give them to me, I listened to that drummer instead, as you must have found out. It's best that it happened when it did."

She faced him. "I'm sorry, Jim. I guess I hurt you, and you didn't deserve to be hurt."

"The drummer?" he asked. "Where is he?"

The girl shrugged. "He meant nothing to me. He was just a means of getting away from Cheyenne."

"From me, you mean," he said unevenly. "Are you —did you get a divorce?"

"No," she admitted. "I guess I never really thought about it. Is that what you want, Jim?"

The door opened behind him, and Dave Thompson said, "Now this is real cozy"

## *Three*

Mace Bowman was up at the first faint flush of dawn the following morning, a Sunday, waiting for the inevitable visit Juan El Pardo would pay the small border town. Early as he was, he found Dave Thompson moving restlessly about the small office when he arrived at the jail. Bowman wasted no words when he saw the gunman.

"Thompson, if you as much as breathe heavy while El Pardo is in town, I'll plant a bullet under your hide!" he warned harshly. "I'll not have Jurado turned into a graveyard so you can pick up a bounty."

The gunman held up his hand placatingly, although the sheriff's blunt tone awoke a smoldering resentment within him.

"Simmer down, Sheriff," he advised coolly. "I'm ridin' along the river with Maxine this mornin'; nothin' more."

"You're stayin' right here until El Pardo rides in and out again," Bowman replied stonily.

Thompson opened his lips to make a quick retort, thought better of it and lowered himself into a chair near the desk. This long-legged galoot wants me to back myself into a corner where I'll have to use a gun to get out, he thought grimly. But not yet, not until I'm sure about that draw of his.

He said amiably, "Sure, Bowman," but his eyes belied the suave tone of his words.

The sun was little more than an hour above the eastern horizon when Juan El Pardo appeared at the west end of the long, dusty street. Behind him rode more than thirty of his *vaqueros*, all heavily armed and grimvisaged. Thompson watched their approach from the window of the office and moved restlessly in his chair. He had not anticipated the large number of riders with El Pardo, and he knew he would be is a hopeless position if the Mexican elected to move against him.

El Pardo held up his hand, and the silent band of horsemen drew rein in front of the sheriff's office. The slender Mexican leader waited impassively for the lawman to put in an appearance.

When Bowman reached the edge of the boardwalk,

El Pardo said evenly, "I've come for Rafael."

"I've been expecting you, *amigo*," Bowman greeted him somberly. "You'll find your cousin at Doc Jarrett's. We did what we could for him, but he died just before dawn."

The Mexican asked stolidly, "Where is this peace officer who shot him down?"

"I want no trouble, *amigo*," Bowman said evenly. "I looked into this matter myself, and witnesses say your cousin went for his gun first."

"I bring no trouble—this time," El Pardo said coolly. "I want only to see the man who shot my cousin, a boy who has never drawn his gun against a man before."

Inside the dim recesses of the office, Dave Thompson breathed a sigh of relief as the Mexican's words reached him. A greedy man, and unscrupulous, he still had no intention of sacrificing his life to gain a paltry five hundred dollars, not when he was sure he had everything to gain by waiting. His plans, carefully formulated during his short stay in Jurado, would, if they worked out, make Stillman's bounty money seem as unimportant as a grain of sand in a dust storm.

Out on the boardwalk, Bowman called, "Thompson!" over his shoulder, and the big gunman appeared in the doorway of the office. Juan El Pardo studied him for several moments without speaking, his dark eyes cold and distant. Then he moved his hand, and the horsemen paced slowly along the street toward Jarrett's office.

Behind him, Dave Thompson threw back his head and laughed. "So that's the big bad wolf who's been scaring the pants off Stillman! Why, that Mexican didn't have the sand to make a play for me with thirty riders at his back!"

Bowman turned at the edge of the boardwalk.

"I don't reckon you did much laughin' when those *vaqueros* rode in," he said curtly, his voice heavy with sarcasm. "You were a big man again when you heard El Pardo give his word not to start trouble."

Thompson flushed, and the sheriff knew his words had come close to the truth. He brushed past the gunman and entered the office.

"El Pardo wanted to take a good look at you," Bowman said pointedly. "When he figures out why you killed Rafael, he'll know the right gent to come after."

Thompson grinned slyly. "Maybe you could tell him why I shot his cousin."

"I could," Mace Brown agreed. "But he'll know soon enough."

Juan El Pardo stayed in town only long enough to claim the body of his slain cousin. Bowman leaned in the doorway of the sheriff's office and watched the cold-eyed rancher ride from Jurado at the head of his *vaqueros.*

Later, he wandered away from the jail and walked toward the converted saloon where the Reverend Jack Benteen held his Sunday morning revivals.

Bowman eased through the door of the old saloon and dropped quietly into a chair at the rear of the long room, but his entrance did not go unobserved by the padre, who promptly interrupted his sermon to make note of the occasion.

"It is men like our sheriff, now entering our humble temple of worship, who have earned our most fervent prayers and support," he boomed out. "Mace Brown, in his capacity as a lawman, stands like a mighty bulwark between the honest citizens of Jurado and those jackals of treachery, Don Stillman, Virgil Storey, Ford Wilson and all their unholy comrades!"

Bowman smiled inwardly at the audacity of the speaker. Benteen apparently cared little that the three men he had just thoroughly castigated were seated at one side of the room, glowering furiously.

Benteen, apparently satisfied for the moment with

the impact of his words, immediately swung back into his sermon. Bowman leaned back in his chair and closed his eyes, strangely relaxed and at peace as he always was in the presence of the tall padre. He heard Benteen's booming voice, but the words were blurred and lost in the maze of his own thoughts.

At last Benteen, lowering his voice to a whisper, quietly intoned a closing prayer, and the fifty or more men and women who had gathered to listen to his words began drifting from the improvised church. Lucy Jensen, an attractive widow in her early thirties and the proprietress of one of the better rooming houses in the town, stopped beside Mace Bowman's chair.

"I'm expecting you for dinner today, Mace," she said in her soft voice, and Bowman thought: a soothing voice, like gentle hands on a fevered brow.

He climbed awkwardly to his feet. "I've been lookin' forward to it all week, Lucy. No one cooks an apple pie or a slab of beef like you."

He watched the trim figure of the widow as she walked away. A hand touched his shoulder, and he turned.

Mace Bowman was an inch or two over six feet, but the Reverend Jack Benteen towered over him by at least four inches.

"Lucy is a very attractive woman," Benteen observed. "A man could do much worse."

Bowman grinned up at the towering padre.

"You're lookin' for marryin' business," he accused him good-naturedly. "Collections must be mighty poor lately."

Don Stillman came up to where they stood, his lips set in a smile but his eyes cold and aloof.

"I enjoyed your sermon, padre," he remarked. "But the side remarks were not appreciated by any of us."

He dipped into his vest pocket and dropped a gold coin into the collection box still held in Benteen's huge hands.

"Maybe the Bible says something about loose talk," he suggested thinly. "Look it up, padre."

Stillman spun on his heel and walked away. Benteen, a big grin on his face, plucked the gold coin from the collection plate and called, "Mr. Stillman!"

The land speculator stopped and turned. Benteen held up the coin for him to see.

"I thank you, and the Lord thanks you," the padre said solemnly. "Rest assured, Brother Stillman, that this money will be put to good purpose!"

He dropped the coin back into the plate. "The good Lord will not object if I use the Devil's own strength against him!"

Stillman flushed angrily and stamped from the building. Mace Bowman shook his head worriedly.

"Padre, you're stirrrin' up a hornet's nest," he warned. "A lot of folks are listenin' to you rip Stillman and his bunch, and he's not the man to let it pass."

"It's not likely he will," Benteen agreed. "But I'm doing what I have to, Mace. Don Stillman has robbed and cheated and bought his way far too long here in the border country. Jurado is not a fit place for men and women to raise their families, and won't be as long as Stillman holds the reins."

Bowman said, "It could cost you a bullet in the back to force his hand, padre."

Benteen was silent for a moment, searching for the right words.

"I reckon I'm no different from other folks," he admitted at last. "I don't want to die, Mace. Maybe there was a time when it didn't matter much, but now I have my work, God's work, and many things to atone for. But you've stood up against Stillman for years, and it's time you had a little help.

Bowman said with a trace of bitterness in his voice, "What good has it done, padre? He still runs Jurado and the border country."

The padre laid a comforting hand on the lawman's shoulder. "Believe me, my friend, it would have been far worse without your hand on the halter; only the good Lord knows how much worse."

Bowman patted his holstered gun. "Stillman is a little leery of the law I carry on my hip, padre. But it won't last forever."

"All the more reason we should act now."

"You're gamblin' everything on the chance Stillman will make a slip when you force his hand. It's too big a risk."

He turned away.

"Do me a favor, padre," he said over his shoulder. "Ride a little easier for a few days; long enough for the folks to savvy what you're tryin' to do."

Mace Bowman was seated at his desk idly leafing through an old stack of wanted posters when Don Stillman came in.

"Howdy, Sheriff," he greeted Mace. "Looks like you're mighty busy this morning."

Bowman returned bluntly, "I look through these wanted posters six times a day, Stillman, hopin' I'll run across one for you."

The land speculator scowled. "I hear your friend El

Pardo was in town this morning."

Bowman grunted but said nothing. Stillman pulled a chair around with the toe of a polished boot and dropped into it. "That Mexican bandit won't be thumbing his nose at the law much longer, Sheriff. Judge Murphy will be issuing a warrant for his arrest first thing in the morning. A murder warrant!"

Mace Bowman looked up from the papers in front of him, asking sharply, "Whose murder?"

"Murders," Stillman corrected himself smugly. "The murders of John Navarre and Ben Gates."

"You must be off your rocker, Stillman. No one can say if those two hombres are alive or dead."

"They would have turned up by now if they were alive."

"Maybe so, but it still doesn't prove El Pardo had anything to do with it."

"Sheriff, everyone knows El Pardo has threatened to burn Jurado to the ground if certain men are not turned over to him. Two of those men were Navarre and Gates."

Bowman's laugh was harsh. "Even supposin' El Pardo could be brought in, and that's supposin' a heck of a lot, you'll never hold him on those charges."

The land speculator shrugged carelessly. "Judge

Murphy thinks we have a case against him."

"Murphy thinks the way you want him to think!" Bowman retorted. "One thing for sure, Stillman: you'll never get away with a rigged trial, not with fifty of El Pardo's *vaqueros* sittin' in the courtroom. Murphy may have some reason to want to please you, but he won't be stupid enough to put his own head in a noose."

The lawyer removed a leather case from an inside pocket and carefully selected an expensive cigar. "I'll expect you to serve the warrant, Sheriff."

"You figure on bein' in the posse if I go after him?"

"Why should I?" Stillman asked easily. "I've never claimed to be a gunslick. You can find plenty of men willing to earn a dollar for a job like that."

"I reckon you know all about hirin' guns," the lawman returned coldly. "You've done enough of it. But take my word for it, Stillman: it'll take more than a few silver dollars to buy the kind of sand it will take to buck El Pardo in his own bailiwick."

He left his chair and moved to the open doorway. "Saw you in church today, Stillman. I wouldn't want anything to happen to Jack Benteen; no floggin's, no fatal accidents, no shootin's. Keep it in mind."

He stepped out on the boardwalk without waiting for an answer and walked aimlessly about the small town, finally turning in at the Maverick. Mike Collins was behind the long bar and nodded a friendly greeting as the lawman approached.

He placed a glass and bottle on the bar, pouring out a drink. "On the house, Mace."

Bowman laid a silver dollar on the bar.

"Might have to close you up one of these days." He smiled. "Wouldn't want a free drink to stand in the way of my duty. And remember, Mike, you work for Don Stillman."

"I work for him, but he doesn't own me," Collins growled. "I'm gettin' mighty tired of his high-handed methods."

Bowman was lifting the amber fluid to his lips when the glass was suddenly jarred from his hand. Whiskey spattered over the front of his clothing as the glass struck the bar and shattered.

"You need the whole bar, you clumsy ox?" a voice snarled at his elbow.

Without turning, Bowman pulled a soiled bandana from his pocket and swabbed at his whiskey-stained shirt. A hand grasped him roughly by the arm and spun him around. He stumbled, half-falling against the bar.

"I asked you a question, mister!"

The lawman pushed away from the bar and calmly

studied the speaker. Of medium height, smooth-faced and hard-eyed, he appeared to be no more than twenty or twenty-one. But the six-gun strapped low on his thigh left little doubt as to his profession.

"Son," Mace advised coolly, "you'd best turn around and head out of here, pronto."

The gunslick moved a step back down the bar. "You're the law around here, and maybe that gives you the right to do a lot of pushin'."

Mike Collins said disgustedly, "Paddle his behind and throw him out of here, Mace!"

The cold eyes of the gunman rested briefly on the barkeep. "Your turn will come, mister. In a minute."

Collins' hands lifted above the level of the bar, and he rested a sawed-off shotgun on its surface. "Any time, bucko! Any time."

"No one is pushin' you around, son," Bowman intervened. "Seems to me you're doin' all the pushin'. Might be a little hard to spend what Stillman is payin' you in Boot Hill."

"Who's Stillman?" the gunman rasped, but the slight color creeping across his face belied his words. "You bumped me, and I don't take that from anyone!"

Bowman pushed his hat to the back of his head. "I'll tell you once more, son. Turn around and walk out of here—while you can."

The young gunman hesitated for a split-second; then his hand dropped to his hip, clawing for the fancy pearl-inlaid butt of his six-gun. He was reasonably fast, a little better than average, but far too slow for the cool-eyed border lawman. Bowman's weapon was out and leveled before the startled newcomer's gun left its holster.

Sweat spurted on the gunman's forehead, and from behind him Mike Collins called out, "Pull it all the way, you two-bit gunslinger! Then you can brag in Hades how you met up with Mace Bowman and he nudged you across the line!"

The stranger released the butt of his gun as if it had suddenly become too hot to handle.

"Mace Bowman!" he croaked. "They told me—"

His lips clamped shut and he watched the lanky sheriff through sullen eyes.

"They told you I was a dodderin' old man who couldn't hit the side of a barn if I was standin' inside it," Bowman guessed, grinning.

The gunman nodded. "I'm ridin' out, Sheriff, but not before I settle a score."

Bowman appraised the stranger, an odd glint in his eyes. Maybe this kid— He shook his head.

"Forget it, son. There's at least a half-dozen gents in this town who could shade your draw and put you in Boot Hill."

"I'll take my chances."

"No."

"You don't owe me a thing, Sheriff. I would have gunned you down if I could."

"I know, but you haven't got what it takes to play a hand in this game, kid," Bowman said brutally. "Lay your gun on the bar and fork your cayuse. If ever you get a hankerin' to ride back to Jurado, keep in mind I draw dry on a man but once."

After a moment's hesitation, the gunman dropped his weapon on the bar and spun on his heel. Bowman watched him walk stiff-legged from the saloon, then holstered his six-gun and poured another drink.

Dave Thompson rode leisurely along the river, to the west, after he had left Maxine a mile or so back to return to Jurado alone.

He topped a low rise, and a scattered group of white-washed buildings came into view a short distance ahead of him. El Pardo's hacienda, he thought. The many spacious ranch buildings were surrounded by a high adobe wall, broken only by a huge double gate facing the north and a smaller one on the south wall. Buildings and wall alike had been freshly whitewashed and gleamed with stark purity under the brilliant sun.

The gunman's preoccupation with the breath-taking beauty of the scene almost proved his undoing. Behind him a harsh voice called, "Steady, mister! One sudden move will be your last!"

Cursing softly at his brief lapse of vigilance, the gunman hesitated for a moment, weighing his chances, then raised his hands chest high.

The stranger ordered sharply, "Turn your horse, slow!"

Bringing his mount around slowly and carefully, Thompson heard the unknown rider exclaim sourly, "It's you! What the devil are you doin' out here, Thompson?"

The gunman watched in silence as Nick Valdes slid the rifle back into its saddle sheath. He returned mildly, "Reckon I could ask you the same thing."

"Just makin' certain I don't wind up like Gates and Navarre," Valdes growled. "Count yourself lucky it wasn't one of El Pardo's riders holdin' this rifle on your back."

Thompson was coolly studying the rancher, whom he had last seen in Don Stillman's office, and suddenly saw a use for him. Heeling his horse forward, he pulled past Valdes. Then his six-gun was in his hand and he was grinning at the startled rider.

"Now I see how easy it is for El Pardo to corral you gents," he remarked. "You're too trustin'."

Valdes finally found his voice. He sputtered angrily, "Stillman will hear about this!"

"More than likely," the gunman agreed ambiguously.

He pulled a leather (throng) from his belt as he stepped from the saddle. "Put your hands behind your back and be mighty careful while you're doin' it!"

He quickly secured the hands of the indignant rancher and remounted. Catching up the reins of Valdes' horse, he swung around and headed back along the river, in the general direction of Jurado.

## Four

Juan El Pardo sat on the cool veranda of his hacienda, staring morosely over the high adobe wall of the courtyard to the lush green fields beyond. A black-haired, slender man of twenty-five, the bronze-hued, symmetrical lines of his face showed unmistakably the influence of his gentle Spanish mother. It was his eyes, dark and brooding, which caught and held the attention of others; eyes reflecting in their depths the fierce Yaqui blood of his father's people.

It was this Yaqui heritage which gave him his determination to fight against the injustices Don Stillman had inflicted upon the Mexican ranchers, and it was this same blood which directed his bitter course of action: give no quarter and expect none.

The soft, reproving words of his mother and the tearful pleading of Marguerita Cardenas, his intended, could not swerve him from his purpose; the proud Spanish blood flowing through his veins made honor as necessary as life itself.

The slim Mexican watched idly as scores of heavily armed *vaqueros* moved slowly about the courtyard or crouched on their heels in the cooling shadows of the wall.

Marguerita Cardenas appeared on the veranda from the dim recesses of the house, and Juan El Pardo quickly leaped to his feet, courteously handing her into a chair. Dark-haired and olive-skinned, the pure Spanish blood of her ancestors apparent in every lithe motion, the girl was stunningly beautiful. But her eyes were shadowed and troubled, and she shuddered visably when she looked at the many *vaqueros* gathered in the courtyard.

El Pardo said gently, "You are unhappy, Marguerita. It grieves me deeply to see you this way."

The girl smiled faintly, but only with her lips.

"Give up this madness, Juan," she said softly, pleadingly. "It can only lead to heartache and sorrow."

El Pardo's eyes were coldly aloof. "Would you have me forget and forgive the murderers of my father? Would you have me cast aside the honor of my hacienda?"

The girl sighed.

"What is honor, if the man I love is in his grave?" she asked reasonably. "If this honor of which you speak must be bought with the blood of my beloved and many of his people, then I say to cast it aside!"

"I cannot forsake my friends, my relatives, and welcome with open arms the mad beast who has already murdered many of my people and who would now steal my hacienda!"

"Your friends and relatives did not fight for their lands," she returned quietly. "They fled below the border, like the lamb before the wolf."

"Because they had no leader!" he cried quickly. "Now I, El Pardo, have taken up their fight, and they flock to my side in hope and faith. Look!"

His hand swept out before him, the gesture encompassing the heavily armed *vaqueros* within the walled courtyard.

"Each day brings more of my people," he told her exultantly, "with guns and horses and ammunition. Soon our might will be greater than our enemies', and they will not stand against us!"

"But the courts of the land say *Señor* Stillman is in the right," the girl protested. "He will send for many men and guns, and his people will give him armies with which to fight."

El Pardo laughed, and the harshness of the sound turned many eyes in the direction of the veranda.

"All the border country knows that what Don Stillman says, Judge Murphy does," he pointed out. "I am not afraid of the soldiers, Marguerita, for they are many miles away. If they come at all, they will come too late to be of help to this jackal!"

The girl laid her hand on his arm, exerting a gentle pressure.

"Let us not quarrel, Juan," she pleaded. "You will do what you must, I know, and that is as it should be. I will always be waiting for you, no matter where your journey ends!"

A movement in the trees beyond the green fields caught El Pardo's attention, and he watched with interest as a large band of horsemen emerged from the heavy growth less than a mile from the hacienda. They reined to a stop in the shadows of the trees and apparently were studying the approaches to the hacienda. At last a rider broke away from the others and rode slowly toward the big gate in the center of the north wall. When the strange horseman was still several hundred yards away, El Pardo raised his hand in a signal, and a *vaquero* standing near the gate touched the brim of his

hat with his fingers. Raising his rifles and sighting carefully, he sent a warning shot inches over the head of the
oncoming rider. Without stopping, the horseman calmly reached behind him and removed a white cloth from
his saddlebags, waving it several times high over his
head.

El Pardo barked out a command, and the big gates
swung open. Then he turned to the girl.

"Please leave me for a few minutes, my dear," he
said softly.

She nodded graciously, and the Mexican helped her
to her feet. He promised, "I will come to you shortly."

El Pardo watched as the graceful *señorita* curtsied
and disappeared into the dim interior of the house.
Then he turned and strode purposefully toward the
gates, reaching them just as the horseman reined his
mount to a stop. His eyes lighted as he recognized his
visitor.

"Welcome to the El Pardo hacienda," he said warm-
ly. "It is always a pleasure to see you again, Mace.
Why did you not bring your friends with you?"

Mace Bowman stepped from the saddle and tossed
the reins to a waiting *vaquero*. "It's their choice, *amigo*.
Reckon they didn't know for sure how you might take
our little visit."

El Pardo asked shrewdly, "Then it's trouble you bring, my friend?"

"You could call it that," the lanky sheriff admitted. He pulled a folded paper from an inner pocket. "This is a warrant chargin' you with kidnapping and murder, Juan. They say you're the gent responsible for whatever happened to Ben Gates and John Navarre."

The wiry Mexican smiled. "You are indeed a brave man, *amigo!* You would take El Pardo from under a hundred guns!"

Bowman glanced around the courtyard and said wryly, "I reckon I won't be takin' you unless you decide to come peaceably."

"If I go with you in peace, will it make the rope less tight around my neck?" El Pardo asked evenly.

Bowman rubbed the side of his jaw, not meeting the Mexican's eyes. "For what it's worth, there's no real evidence against you."

"Then why was the warrant for my arrest issued?" the Mexican asked bluntly.

Bowman said quietly, "You know the answer to that as well as I."

"I have your word El Pardo would receive a fair trial?"

The lawman shook his head. "I can't give you my

word, *amigo*. If you stand trial in Judge Murphy's court, chances are you'll hang."

El Pardo scowled. "You wish to take me to certain death?"

"That's not what I said," Bowman retorted. "It's my duty to take you back to Jurado, if I can. It goes no farther than that."

The slim Mexican said thoughtfully, "You have always been known to me as a fair man, *Señor* Bowman. If you were El Pardo, and I wore the sheriff's badge, would you ride back to Jurado with me?"

Bowman replied shortly, "No."

El Pardo smiled grimly. "Then surely you do not expect me to answer Judge Murphy's summons?"

"I've never taken you for a fool."

"Then why did you make the long ride to the El Pardo hacienda?"

"I came as a friend," Bowman replied evenly, "to ask you to leave the border country and go below the river before it's too late. You've been wronged and you want justice, but you'll only find it in a court of law, not in bloodshed and violence."

With a wave of his hand El Pardo indicated the sullen-faced *vaqueros* in the courtyard.

"I am strong enough to move against Don Stillman

now," he boasted. "And there are many more *vaqueros* riding to my side each day."

The lawman nodded his agreement. "You're strong today, and maybe you'll be even stronger tomorrow, Juan. For a few weeks, maybe even a month or two, you and your *vaqueros* could ride mighty tall in the saddle. But the end would come, and with it, the end of El Pardo and his hacienda."

"You are thinking of the gringo army," the Mexican guessed. "But it would come too late to save Don Stillman."

"More than likely you're right," the lawman admitted. "But the soldiers would not allow you to live in peace above the river, *amigo*. If you move against Stillman, a lot of innocent folks will be killed, and the army will hang you just as high as Stillman would."

He jerked his head in the direction of the *vaqueros*. "Look at the riders you call your friends, *amigo*. Some are friends, sure; some are relatives you can trust. But the rest of them are scum from both sides of the border, outlaws, wanted men, riffraff who would as soon stab you in the back as look at you. They're here for one reason—loot—not for friendship or because they want to help you in your fight against Stillman.

"Once you turn them loose against Jurado, your control over them will be gone and they'll react like the scum they are. You'll have to stand by and watch folks you've known most of your life slaughtered and tortured because they happen to live in the same town as Don Stillman. But in the end, the soldiers will take your hacienda from you, piece by piece if they have to, and stretch your neck on the nearest cottonwood tree."

El Pardo shook his head. "You are wrong, my friend. My *vaqueros* are loyal and will obey me. I will not permit useless slaughter."

Bowman said grimly, "We'll see."

El Pardo studied the sheriff, a slight frown creasing his forehead. "I know you speak as a friend, *amigo*, but my decision is made. I will not leave the lands of my people; I cannot, with honor. And if you would take me back to Jurado, you must be prepared to fight!"

Bowman took the reins from the hands of the silent *vaquero* and stepped into the saddle.

"This makes you an outlaw, legal game for every bounty hunter along the border," he warned. "I reckon that's what Stillman had in mind from the start. He knew you couldn't be convicted in any court of law except Murphey's, but with a price on your head—"

He shrugged his broad shoulders.

"I do not live in fear of Stillman or his bounty hunters," El Pardo said proudly. He reached inside his jacket and held out a slip of paper to the lawman. Bowman, glancing at the paper, saw that it was identical with the one he had seen in Don Stillman's office, with one exception.

Dave Thompson's name had been added to El Pardo's list of wanted men!

Bowman removed his hat and wiped the moisture from his face. "There are too many names here, Juan. You forgot to scratch out Nick Valdes' name."

El Pardo looked puzzled. "Valdes? I know nothing of Nick Valdes."

The lawman eyed the Mexican warily. "Valdes turned up missing this mornin'. Hasn't been seen since early yesterday mornin'."

El Pardo called out a command, and a swarthy, thick-set *vaquero* ran up. The two men talked excitedly for several minutes; then the Mexican leader dismissed the rider.

"We know nothing of the disappearance of *Señor* Valdes," El Pardo said emphatically. "All of our *vaqueros* have been accounted for, and none left the hacienda yesterday."

Bowman asked, "Who, then?"

El Pardo shrugged. "A coyote is not known for his

courage. Perhaps *Señor* Valdes disappeared of his own choice."

He pointed to the list still in the hands of the lawman. "You must deliver those jackals into my hands by sundown tomorrow, *amigo*. It is the only way Jurado will be permitted to stand."

Bowman's face was bleak. "And if the town will not give them up?"

"Then I will lead my *vaqueros* into Jurado!"

Bowman said coldly, "We've been friends for many years, *amigo*, but if your *vaqueros* spill one drop of blood in Jurado, my first bullet will be aimed at your heart!"

Lifting his hand in a brief salute, he wheeled and rode slowly through the big gates.

When he and his men reached the small border town some time later, the posse drifted apart, with Dave Thompson heading for the Maverick and Bowman pulling up at the jail. Inside, he circled the corner of his desk and slumped wearily into his chair.

Denver Rogers asked, "You come up with El Pardo?"

Bowman nodded. "I talked to him. We're in for some mighty rough goin'."

Briefly he sketched the details of his visit to El Pardo's hacienda. Then he said, "Skedaddle over to the land office and get Stillman. I want to see him, pronto."

When the irate land office man finally put in an appearance some twenty minutes later, Bowman was still seated behind his desk, long legs stretched out across the top. Stillman glared angrily.

"Are you so busy you can't come to my office when you want to see me?" he barked. "Maybe you have time to sit around, but I'm a busy man!"

Bowman said evenly, "If I were you, Stillman, I'd bundle up what work you have in a gunny sack and head for the mesquite, unless you're hankerin' to meet up with your three pards."

"I won't allow that Mexican bandit to scare me out of town!" the lawyer snapped testily.

Bowman tossed the list of names across the desk to the land speculator. "El Pardo gives the town until tomorrow night to hand over you jaspers, or he'll come after you."

As Stillman examined the list, Bowman added, "There's no way we can stop him if he elects to move in on the town."

Stillman's face reflected the emotions boiling up inside him.

"El Pardo is howling at the moon," he said at last,

but there was little conviction in his voice. "If he tries taking Jurado with the twenty or thirty riders siding him, we'll drive him into the dust!"

"I saw maybe a hundred *vaqueros* at El Pardo's hacienda, and enough guns for that many more," Bowman said somberly. "Not cowhands, Stillman, but hardcases, gunhands and the like; the kind that's been raidin' and burnin' and sackin' on both sides of the border for twenty years or more. They won't be stopped with a law book and a crooked judge, mister!"

He glanced through the dusty window and saw a crowd slowly collecting in the street outside the jail. When he reached the door, Stillman was a step behind him, and he heard the lawyer draw a sharp breath when he saw the fifty or more men and women circling uneasily a few yards away.

Stillman asked in a low voice, "What does it mean, Sheriff?"

Mace Bowman pushed his hat to the back of his head. "It's my guess the posse has been doing a little talkin', Stillman. Maybe these folks want to talk about you and your pards."

Stillman snorted his contempt as Gil Sheldon, a member of the posse that morning, moved clear of the others.

"Sheriff," he called, "these folks want to know the straight of all this talk about El Pardo sackin' the town."

Bowman nodded. "I reckon that's their right, Gil." Speaking in a loud, clear voice, he outlined El Pardo's demands.

"We can't stop him if he elects to send his *vaqueros* against the town," he concluded. "He has too many guns, too many riders."

He said in a low voice over his shoulder, "Get inside, Stillman," and heard the land speculator retreating into the shadows of the office.

Sheldon was apparently acting as spokesman for the crowd. He advanced within twenty feet of the lawman, a scowl on his face.

"We've talked this thing over, Mace," he said loudly. "We say to give El Pardo the coyotes who've been robbin' the Mexicans blind all these years. We don't reckon we belong in this fight."

Bowman replied evenly, "You all know what may happen to these men, and probably will, if you turn them over to El Pardo?"

A woman called, "What happens to *us* if we don't give them up? Will El Pardo keep his promise and burn the town?"

Bowman said carefully, "I don't think there's any doubt but what he'll sack and burn the town, as he says he will."

"Will he leave the rest of us alone?"

"Someone's bound to be hurt if El Pardo turns his *vaqueros* loose on the town."

"What about the soldiers?" another questioned.

"It's too late for the army," the lawman replied. "The nearest post is well over two hundred miles away. They couldn't get here in time to do us any good."

"We all know why El Pardo is on the warpath," Sheldon called. "I reckon there's not a man standin' here right now who wouldn't do the same thing if some jasper killed his kin-folk and tried to take over his land!"

"What would you do?" the woman who had spoken before called again.

Bowman mopped his face with the wrinkled bandana.

"This is your town and I work for you," he evaded. "I reckon it's up to you whether you elect to fight or give El Pardo what he wants."

"What about the law, Mace? Would we be breakin' it?"

"You all know there's not much book law along the border," Bowman returned carefully. "Mostly it's what a man thinks is right and what he thinks is wrong. Maybe a court back east would say you'd be wrong in givin' up Stillman and the others. I don't know."

Sheldon shouted, "Back east Stillman wouldn't get away with the things he has here, Sheriff! And we wouldn't have to worry about anyone slaughtering our families!"

Bowman nodded his agreement. "I won't argue the point with you, Gil. I can't make the decision for you."

"Then give us Stillman," Sheldon said roughly. "We know he's in the office behind you. We'll round up the rest of his gang and turn them over to El Pardo."

"It's my job," Bowman replied quietly. "If the town decides to give them up, I'll handle it in my own way."

"We'll take the chore off your hands," Sheldon insisted.

"I don't want any trouble with you, Gil," the lawman said coldly, "but no one is goin' to handle my job for me?"

"How do we know you'll turn them over to El Pardo?"

"It's the chance you'll have to take."

He turned to the others standing silently behind Sheldon. "You all know I don't like what Stillman's been doin' any more than you do. But as long as I'm the law in this town, I'll not stand for a mob steppin' in!"

Gil Sheldon glanced around him and saw enough friendly faces to give him courage.

"Maybe we can take care of that, too," he suggested slyly. "Give him up, Mace, while you can."

Bowman warned harshly, "Don't do anything foolish, Gil!"

Sheldon raised his hand in a signal to the others. Bowman took one step backward, drawing his six-gun and firing in the same smooth motion. The high heel of Sheldon's right boot disappeared in a puff of dust, and he staggered drunkenly, falling flat on his back in the street. He was up quickly, dust-coated and blustering, but studiously avoiding any movement toward his own weapon.

Bowman swung the muzzle of his gun back and forth in a short arc. "There's five bullets left in this gun, folks. Take the time to figure out which five of you won't be eatin' supper with your families if you try to get past me."

The near-mob began breaking up and drifting away. Mace Bowman released a deep breath as he watched them go, then spun on his heel and re-entered the jail. Stillman was seated on a corner of the desk, a worried frown wrinkling his brow.

He asked sharply, "What are you going to do about this, Sheriff?"

The land speculator saw the answer in Mace's eyes before he spoke. "If you and your pards are in town tomorrow mornin', chances are I'll turn you over to El Pardo. Those people you saw out there will be back, and I reckon they'll want your hides."

"You can't do that, Sheriff!" Stillman exclaimed, dismayed. "It would be nothing short of murder!"

"It would be murder if I didn't!" Bowman retorted. "A lot of innocent folks will die for what you and your pards have done."

Without another word, Stillman almost ran from the office. Bowman grinned mirthlessly as he watched him go. Unless he missed his guess, neither Stillman or any of the others would be around when the town made its decision.

The sheriff settled his hat firmly on his head and stepped out on the boardwalk. The disappearance of Nick Valdes bothered him, and he had a question or two to ask.

In the Maverick, Collins came up quickly, and Bowman asked, "Dave Thompson been around?"

"He was here about twenty minutes ago, Mace," Collins told him. "He left about the time the ruckus started in front of your office."

The burly, granite-faced bartender swabbed at the surface of the bar with a damp, foul-smelling rag. "That gent's a queer duck for a peace officer, Mace. Doggone if he wasn't one of those hollering the loudest for you to turn Stillman and his bunch over to El Pardo."

"A foolish thing, considerin' he's on that list," Bowman agreed. "But maybe he doesn't know that."

Maxine came down the long stairway, and the lawman moved his head briefly in greeting. The girl came up to where he was standing.

"Hello, Mace." She smiled.

"You're a mighty pretty little filly today," the lawman observed critically. "Dave Thompson put those stars in your eyes?"

Faint color touched the girl's cheeks. "Maybe."

"Maxine, you rode out of Jurado with Dave Thompson yesterday mornin'," he said, "along the river. You didn't ride back with him."

The girl glanced at him curiously. "My, what sharp eyes you have!"

"Part of my job."

"Maybe I think I'm old enough to ride alone," she suggested, a little annoyed.

"Sure," Bowman agreed. "Where did Thompson go after he left you?"

She shrugged her shoulders. "Why not ask him?"

"I'm askin' you," Bowman returned evenly.

"I don't really know," the girl said truthfully. "Dave asked about the El Pardo hacienda, and I told him how to get there. He was still by the river when I last saw him."

Her eyes were troubled when she looked up at him. "Why are you asking all these questions, Mace?"

"No reason," the lawman said shortly, turning away. As he reached the door, he checked his stride to allow Jim Kerby to enter the saloon.

## Five

Darkness fell swiftly, a soft, velvety blanket effectively concealing the drab ugliness of the small border town.

Mace Bowman, strangely restless, paced slowly through the darkened streets. In front of the Maverick, Manuel Hernandez called softly, "Good evening, *Señor* Bowman," and Bowman stopped near the chair of the blind Mexican *vaquero*.

"Howdy, Manuel."

"Jurado is unhappy tonight," the Mexican ventured. "Fear is heavy upon the shoulders of our neighbors."

"They've a right to be scared," Bowman returned. "El Pardo is holdin' all the aces in this game."

"I find it hard to believe Juan will carry out his threat," Manuel said, troubled. "He is a gentle man at heart, and kind. The hurt must be very deep to force him to turn to violence."

"He has reason enough, I reckon," Bowman replied. "I like Juan, and I hoped it would never come to this."

He saw the trim figure of Lucy Jensen crossing the dust-laden street toward them, a carefully wrapped parcel in her hands. She was still several yards away when Manuel called courteously, "Good evening, *Señora* Jensen!"

She was laughing and a little breathless when she reached them. "It's uncanny how Manuel can tell who I am even when I'm walking in all that dust!"

Both men smiled, and Bowman said, "I think he recognized you by the smell of that apple pie you're carryin'!"

"Why, it *is* apple pie! For you, Manuel." She laid the parcel in the blind man's lap.

Manuel inclined his head. "Thank you, *señora!* I knew you were baking this afternoon, and selfish as I am, I was hoping you would share your good fortune with me!"

"I hope you like it, Manuel. And now I must hurry back."

As she turned away, Bowman called, "Wait, Lucy! I'll walk you back home."

She said, pleased, "Why, of course, Mace!" and he took her arm as they started across the street. It happened while they were outlined for an instant against the light streaming through the open windows of the Maverick.

A streamer of orange flame lashed out from the mouth of an alley across the street from the saloon, and Bowman heard the sharp report of a six-gun as Lucy Jensen gave a strangled cry and fell against him. There was a second flash, and he heard the angry snap of a heavy caliber bullet as it brushed past his head.

He dropped to the street, cushioning the fall of the stricken woman with his arms and body. The unknown gunman fired again as Bowman rolled away from her, and he triggered two quick shots in return and heard a soft moan of pain. Six-gun ready, he waited for the hidden marksman to reveal his position, but no more shots came. Men began streaming from the saloon behind him, and Bowman hurried to his feet, running to the side of Lucy Jensen.

He knelt and called her name softly, but she was beyond hearing. Someone called in a shocked voice, "There's blood all over the front of her dress!" and Bowman snarled, "Stop the palaverin' and give me a hand!" Eager hands lifted her gently and carried her swiftly to Doc Jarrett's office a few doors from the Maverick.

Bowman waited, grim-faced, for the old doctor to complete his work in the inner room. When he finally re-appeared, the lawman had his answer in Jarrett's solemn face.

His voice was unintentionally harsh as he asked, "How is she, Doc?"

Jarrett said carefully, "Mace, I can't give her any more than a fifty-fifty chance, at best. The bullet struck low on the left shoulder, very close to her heart. An inch lower and—"

He made a futile motion with his hands, and Bowman said, "I'd like to see her."

"Not now, Mace," Jarrett replied. "She's in a coma from shock and loss of blood. If we're lucky, she may be able to talk to you in a day or so."

He shook his head regretfully. "I wish the news could be better, Mace. I just can't understand why anyone would want to shoot Lucy."

"The bullet wasn't meant for her," Bowman said, turning away. "Way it looks, some jasper took a shot at me and missed."

Denver Rogers and Sandy Morgan were waiting for Bowman when he returned to his office.

"Round up all the special deputies you can find," Mace told them harshly. "Take this town apart board by board if you have to, but come up with an hombre with a bullet hole or crease in his carcass. Chances are he'll be the gent we want."

On the second floor of the Maverick, Maxine sat in front of her mirror and dispiritedly dabbed powder on her face. When a knock sounded at the door, she waited apprehensively for a moment, and it came again, louder.

She called, "Who is it?"

"It's me, Dave!"

The dance hall girl moved to the door and slipped the bolt, opening it wide for the gunman. When she saw his bloodstained shirt, she exclaimed, "Dave, what happened?"

"Just a scratch," Thompson said curtly, closing the door and sliding the bolt in place. "I want you to clean it up and put a bandage on it."

"No, Dave!" she said fearfully. "Let Doc Jarrett take care of it for you."

He was visibly annoyed. "It's only a scratch, and I don't want any doctor foolin' with it!"

"If you're in trouble, please tell me about it," Maxine pleaded. "At least fifty people must have seen you come up here, Dave."

"I held my vest over my arm!" he snapped irritably. "No one saw the bloodstains. Now will you bandage it for me?"

She waited as the gunman stripped off his shirt. A bullet had ripped open the flesh of his upper left arm and blood flowed freely, but the wound itself seemed a minor one.

When the girl finished cleaning and bandaging the gash, Thompson picked up the shirt and grimaced when he saw the bloodstains around the rent in the sleeve. He tossed the ruined garment into a corner of the room.

"Reckon you'll have to pick up another shirt in my room in the hotel," he told her.

The gunman held up his hand as the girl threw a light shawl over her shoulders and turned toward the door. He warned, "Nothin' about this to anyone. Nothin' at all."

When the girl returned some time later, she watched with troubled eyes as he struggled into the clean shirt, seeing him wince with pain when he moved his wounded arm.

She said at last, "Do you know what you've done, Dave?"

Thompson finished buttoning his shirt and looked

up. "What are you tryin' to say?"

"When you shot at Mace Bowman tonight, your bullet hit Lucy Jensen," she said soberly. "She may die."

The gunman shook his head, not meeting her eyes. "Don't reckon I know what you're talkin' about."

Maxine turned the lamp low and walked to the window. "Come here, Dave."

When Thompson reached her side, she pointed down into the street. When he looked over her shoulder he saw that the window gave a good view of the street below and the dark mouth of an alley across from the Maverick.

She said bleakly, "I was standing here when the shots were fired."

Thompson backed away, frowning.

"You think you saw something down there, something to do with me," he said brusquely. "What was it, Maxine?"

"Do I have to put it in words, Dave?" the girl asked despairingly.

He reached out and took the girl by the arm, swinging her around so that she faced him. "What do you intend doin' about it?"

Maxine stood looking down at the floor, refusing to meet his eyes. The gunman released his grip on her arm and stepped back.

"Forget what you saw down there, Maxine," he coaxed, but his eyes were cold and deadly. "It'll work out. I promise you."

"But why?" the girl asked, her voice scarcely more than a whisper. "What reason could you possibly have for wanting Mace Bowman dead?"

"The sheriff stands in my way," he said bluntly. "There's a fortune to be had for the askin' in Jurado, and I aim to take my share!"

He glanced at her. "You were the one who warned me against facin' Bowman in an open fight."

"When I said that, I didn't mean that you should ambush him!" the girl said quickly. "Mace has always been good to me, Dave. And now there's Lucy Jensen. What if she dies?"

"It was an accident," he said carelessly. "The bad light threw my aim off a mite, I reckon."

"If Mace Bowman finds out who fired those shots, and he will, you won't be able to run far enough or fast enough to stay ahead of him!"

He grinned evilly. "Bowman won't be botherin' me or anyone else much longer!"

The girl pulled a shawl over her shoulders.

"I've got to go downstairs now," she said. "Killing

doesn't mean much to you, Dave; it's like a game to you. I feel a little sorry for you."

"Don't waste your time feelin' sorry for me!" the gunman retorted. "Just don't do anything *you* might be sorry for. I've come too far to let anyone stand in my way, anyone at all."

The girl felt the cold hand of fear clutching her heart as she left the room and slowly descended the stairway.

West of Jurado, on the outskirts of the El Pardo hacienda, Dave Thompson lay flat on his belly in the high grass on the same rise where he had been accosted by Nick Valdes two days before, powerful field glasses held to his eyes. The object of his attention was a large group of *vaqueros* in the walled courtyard of the hacienda.

The gunman maintained his lonely vigil long after the last of the heavily armed *vaqueros* had filed through the big gates of the courtyard. El Pardo himself headed the largest band of horsemen; smaller groups broke away and rode off in several directions as soon as they had left the walls of the hacienda behind them. Soon all were gone from sight, but still Thompson's eyes remained glued to the field glasses.

At last he rose leisurely to his feet. He had seen two women on the veranda as the riders left the courtyard, and the gunman was certain they were *Señora* El Pardo and the Mexican's beautiful fiancée, Marguerita Cardenas. It was around the woman and the girl that the gunman had laid his plans.

Catching up his horse, he swung into the saddle and rode boldly from the trees toward the distant hacienda. He had little fear of bullets from the walls, certain that the badge pinned to his vest would at least momentarily deter any of the defenders from opening fire on him.

A shot rang out of the still air while he was still several hundred yards from the gates, and the gunman knew a bullet had been fired close to his head. Calmly, as he had watched Mace Bowman do, he pulled a white rag from his saddlebag and waved it over his head. The gates remained closed, but no further shots were fired as he drew near.

A grim-faced *vaquero*, rifle cradled in his arms, watched stonily from behind the gates. He warned, "Come no closer, *señor!*"

Thompson pulled on his reins and stuffed the white cloth back in his saddlebag. "I've come to see *Señora* El Pardo, *amigo*. I have a message from Mace Bowman."

The guard said shortly, "The *señora* sees no one in the absence of her son."

"Tell her Sheriff Bowman sent me," the gunman said confidently. "She'll see me."

"Wait here," the guard instructed stiffly.

Five minutes later, Thompson saw him leave the main house and trot across the courtyard. The cross-bar was lifted and the big gates swung open.

"Leave your mount at the gate!" the guard ordered bluntly as Thompson started for the veranda.

The gunman shrugged and stepped from his saddle, tying the reins to a bar of the gate. There was an exaggerated swagger to his step as he crossed the courtyard, and when he reached the veranda, he bowed with courtesy to the two women seated there.

"Howdy, ladies!"

*Señora* El Pardo looked steadily at him, distaste in her eyes. "Carlos has informed me you are carrying a message from *Señor* Bowman."

The gunman nodded.

"Sheriff Bowman thinks you and the girl should ride into Jurado and stay there until this trouble is over," he lied smoothly. "He don't reckon it's safe for women to be out on the range."

"Why did not *Señor* Bowman bring this message himself?" she demanded. "He knows he is always welcome at the hacienda."

"He's busy," Thompson replied coolly. "A woman stopped a bullet last night in front of the Maverick, and he's tryin' to run down the gent who fired the shot."

"Juan is quite able to take care of his home and family," the *señora* said haughtily. "I deplore the violence and bloodshed which has come to the border country, but we cannot desert our home because of it."

"I reckon you'd best do as the sheriff says," the gunman said curtly. "We expect big trouble along the river any day now."

Dave's tone apparently offended the *señora*.

"Who are you, young man?" she asked sharply. "You are extremely offensive, and I shall speak to *Señor* Bowman regarding it!"

The gunman moved casually to a point back of the girl's chair.

"My moniker is Dave Thompson," he said easily, slipping a knife from his belt and touching the razor-sharp edge to the back of the girl's neck. "And maybe you'd best do as I say. Not likely El Pardo would want anything to happen to his future wife!"

"Thompson!" *Señora* El Pardo exclaimed, her face ashen. "*Señor* Bowman would not have sent you here with a message!"

"Can't see where it makes any difference now," the gunman pointed out. "If you're smart, you'll do exactly as I tell you."

The girl urged, "Summon Carlos, *señora!* I am not afraid of this jackal and his knife!"

Thompson pressed lightly on the knife, and a thin red line appeared on the girl's neck.

"I'll kill you both without battin' an eyelash if it's the difference between a bullet in my head and ridin' out of here," he warned grimly. "If trouble starts, you two will be the first to go. Keep it in mind."

The gunman's cold, expressionless eyes left little doubt in the minds of the two women that he would do exactly as he threatened. The *señora* laid a comforting hand on the arm of the young girl.

"We must do as he says, my dear," she said gently. "This man will not hesitate to spill our blood."

She turned to Thompson. "What is it you wish us to do?"

"Now that's a heap better!" he approved, grinning. "We're goin' to ride out of here, the three of us. Call that dark-skinned servant of yours and have him bring up my horse from the gate. We'll need two more for you and the girl."

Carlos appeared at the *señora's* call and immediately left to carry out her orders. Thompson, keeping a watchful eye on the two women, produced a worn tally book and wrote rapidly for several minutes. Then he ripped the sheet from the book and placed it on the small table at the girl's elbow, weighting it down with a cartridge from his belt.

Carlos came up with the horses, and Thompson whispered, "Send him back to the gate."

The *vaquero* departed, and the gunman hustled the two women into their saddles, then mounted himself and heeled his mount close to his two captives.

"My hand will be on the butt of my gun," he warned. "When we reach the gate, order Carlos to open it and keep right on ridin'. Don't make any mistake, even a small one!"

Carlos was more than a little puzzled by the actions of the three riders, but his training would not allow him to question his mistress' judgment, and he swung open the gates at her command. The three rode beyond the whitewashed walls, and the heavy gates clanged shut behind them.

Thompson guided the women in a northeasterly direction until the hacienda faded from view, then swung east and south toward the river. A short time later all three disappeared into the thick jungle of mesquite bordering the river.

## Six

Mace Bowman was seated behind the battered, boot-scarred desk in his office when Dave Thompson rode into Jurado late that afternoon. The lawman's shrewd eyes observed with interest the dusty, travel-stained clothing of the town marshal.

He remarked dryly, "Seems like you find plenty of reasons to take you out of town these days."

Thompson beat some of the dust from his clothing with the brim of his hat. "Handle your job, Sheriff, and I'll take care of mine!"

"I'll do just that," Bowman agreed mildly, "as long as you savvy your bailiwick is Jurado, not the border country."

The gunman sprawled out in a chair near the door. "Catch up with Stillman and his bunch? Heard the town voted to turn them over to El Pardo."

"Don't forget *your* name is on the list of hombres El Pardo wants," Bowman pointed out. "Maybe you'd best join Stillman and the others out in the mesquite."

"I've a notion El Pardo will forget about that deadline of his," Thompson returned smugly. "Once he studies it out, maybe he'll forget about raidin' the town at all."

Bowman said grimly, "If you think that, you don't know El Pardo."

"I know his breed," the gunman replied coolly. "He'll back off when the chips are down."

He rolled and lit a brown-paper cigarette. He asked idly, "Got any leads on who might have triggered a shot at you last night?"

"I've a notion or two," Bowman told him. "But I'll come up with the answer, bucko. Count on it."

Thompson pushed himself to his feet.

"Sure you will, Sheriff," he said, a faint grin twisting his lips. "See you around."

At dusk a rider slid his mount to a stop in front of the jail and leaped from the saddle. As Bowman hurried from the office he recognized Cliff Anderson, Storey's range boss, his arm still securely trussed in a sling. The lawman noted that Anderson's hip holster was empty, as well as the rifle sheath on his saddle.

"What's the hurry, Cliff?"

"El Pardo cleaned Storey's range as slick as a whistle and burned every building to the ground!" Anderson exclaimed excitedly.

Bowman asked quickly, "Anyone hurt?"

"Only feelin's, I reckon. El Pardo rode in early this mornin' with maybe fifty or sixty riders behind him. We knew we couldn't buck odds like that and stay alive, so we tossed our guns on the ground when he told us to. Took me a while to round up my cayuse after they left."

"Where's Storey?"

Anderson shrugged his shoulders. "Who knows? Some gent rode in late last night, and Storey grabbed a horse and lit out. Haven't seen him since."

After a few more questions, Bowman nodded his head in a gesture of dismissal, and the range foreman headed in the direction of the Maverick. Denver Rogers said worriedly, "I don't like this, Mace!"

"We all saw it comin'," Bowman countered. "There's always a time when payment is due, in either blood or gold."

"El Pardo may end up on the wrong end of the payment," the deputy predicted.

"He's mighty shrewd," Bowman said. "Likely he

figures on sweepin' the range clean while he keeps us boxed up here in Jurado. Knows he's safe as long as word can't leak out about what he's up to."

Bowman rubbed the stiff bristles on the side of his jaw reflectively. "Maybe a single rider can break through El Pardo's *vaqueros* and reach the fort. Be ready to ride out first thing in the mornin'."

The deputy nodded reluctantly. "Mace, El Pardo is a friend of yours!"

"I know," the lawman returned quietly. "I'm not certain El Pardo does!"

He nodded his head in a brief salute and walked slowly along the street. He was a few steps past the Maverick, deep in thought, when it suddenly occurred to him that the interior of the saloon was unusually quiet. Retracing his steps, he peered over the bat-wings.

Dave Thompson was crouched in the center of the room, facing the bar, his hand poised over the butt of his six-gun. In front of him, a young, slender *vaquero* stood transfixed with fear, his arms hanging helplessly at his sides. Twenty feet away, Mike Collins rested a sawed-off shotgun on the polished top of the bar, its black muzzle pointed directly at the gunman's head.

Thompson was saying coldly, "Barkeep, I could drive two bullets through your head before you made up your mind to squeeze that trigger!"

Mace Bowman pushed through the swinging doors into the brightly lighted room. He called sharply, "That's enough!"

Without turning his head, Thompson rasped, "Stay out of this, Sheriff! It's no concern of yours!"

Bowman slid the six-gun from his holster. "I'm makin' it mine, friend!"

Gradually the tension seeped from the gunman's body and he straightened.

"You're a mighty nosy gent, Bowman," he grated, still without looking at the lawman. "Maybe the day will come when that will all be changed!"

Bowman snapped shortly, "Maybe, but if you're lookin' for a quick ride to Boot Hill, just put a hand on that gun!"

Thompson wheeled angrily and left the saloon, keeping his eyes averted as he brushed past the lawman. Bowman watched him go, then stepped up to the bar.

"What's behind this, Mike?"

The bartender, visibly angered by the near-shooting, placed a glass and bottle in front of the sheriff.

"I've watched Thompson mighty close since he shot

Rafael Benavides the other day," Collins explained. "This time I caught him tryin' to pick a gunfight with that younker. Doggone it, Mace, that Mexican isn't even totin' an iron!"

Bowman turned to the frightened vaquero. "Ride out, son, and keep right on ridin'. The marshal may try to follow this up."

After the Mexican scurried from the saloon, Collins said, "Thompson is kill-crazy, Mace!"

Bowman shook his head. "Thompson's done a little killin', and maybe he likes it, but that isn't the reason he tried to prod the Mexican into a gun fight. He's got some reason for wantin' to keep El Pardo stirred up against the town."

Jim Kerby drifted into the saloon and took up a position at the bar. He nodded briefly in Bowman's direction and waited patiently as Collins served him.

"I still think Thompson is loco," the bartender insisted when he stopped in front of Bowman. "Last night he rushed through the back door like a buffaloed steer and ran upstairs. Seems to me he's mighty thick with Maxine for a jasper who's only been here a few days."

"Maxine is a pretty filly," Bowman pointed out. "Only natural Thompson would make a play for her."

"Maybe you're right," Collins said doubtfully. "All

I know is, Thompson stayed up there about an hour, and when he came down again he had on another shirt. I tell you, Mace, there's more to it than meets the eye!"

"Wearin' another shirt?" Bowman repeated, puzzled. "About what time was it, Mike?"

The bartender's brow furrowed in thought. "I reckon I don't rightly know, Mace."

Then he slapped the bar towel against the top of the bar with a soggy thud. "I've got it! It was right after I heard those shots in the street, Mace, when someone tried to shoot you and hit Lucy instead."

"You certain about that shirt?" the lawman asked. When Collins nodded his head emphatically, he added, "Where's Maxine now?"

The bartender pointed with his finger, and Bowman headed for the stairs. He knocked twice, hard, before the girl slid back the bolt and opened the door a few inches.

She said, surprised, "Mace!"

"Expectin' someone else?" Bowman asked evenly. "I won't take up much of your time, Maxine. Just a question or two."

The girl moved aside without speaking, and Bowman entered the softly lighted room. He pushed the door closed with the heel of his boot and leaned a shoulder against it, covertly studying the girl as she moved past him. He waited silently as she drew up a chair before her mirror.

"You'll have to excuse my back, Mace," she said over her shoulder. "I'm due downstairs in a few minutes."

Bowman said abruptly, "Was Dave Thompson here at any time last night?"

The girl, about to apply powder to her face, stopped and met his eyes in the mirror. "Has Dave done anything wrong?"

"Was he here?"

"You know he was, or you wouldn't be asking," she said quietly.

Bowman stepped to the dressing table and turned the lamp up, then returned to his position near the door.

"Anything wrong with him?" he asked casually. "Like a bullet hole, maybe?"

The girl's eyes were cool. "Not that I know of, Mace."

The lawman pointed to the floor at his feet.

"Maybe you cut yourself," he suggested. "Someone wiped up bloodstains here within the last day or two."

"I wouldn't know about that," Maxine said stubbornly. "Maybe the cleaning woman cut herself while she was straightening up. She's usually a little tipsy, you know."

"I know," Bowman agreed. "Then quickly, "Why did Thompson change his shirt while he was up here?"

The dance hall girl was startled by the unexpected question, but she recovered quickly.

"I spilled part of a bottle of cologne on it," she explained glibly. "Dave wouldn't wear the shirt, so I went to his room and got him another. That's all there was to it, Mace."

The girl's brief hesitation convinced Bowman she was lying. "You've been around saloons long enough to know Thompson's kind of man, Maxine. He's a killer, through and through, and he'd put a slug in you without givin' it a second thought if he reckoned you knew enough to put a rope around his neck."

"There's nothing I can tell you," she replied, and Bowman caught the undercurrent of fear in her voice.

He tried again. "Thompson came up here and changed his shirt right after someone took a shot at me and hit Lucy Jensen. I'm mighty certain one of my bullets creased whoever fired that shot."

He moved to the window and looked down into the street. "Anyone standin' here might've seen the whole thing. Maxine, Lucy may die. That mean anything to you?"

She said in a low voice, "I wish I could help you."

Bowman said, "All right," and moved toward the door. When he reached it, he stopped and looked back. "Where is the shirt Dave took off?"

"I'm not sure, but I think he took it with him when he left."

The lawman's shrewd eyes made a rapid inspection of the room; then he nodded and stepped into the corridor. Jim Kerby called to him as he passed through the barroom on his way to the street.

"Belly up and I'll buy one, Mace."

Bowman hesitated for a moment, then nodded his assent. But his manner was cool and distant as he poined the ex-lawman at the bar. He knew Kerby had been following him, watching his every move, but as yet he hadn't figured out why. He sipped the fiery liquor placed before him and waited for Kerby to speak.

"I'm workin' for Stillman," Kerby said suddenly. "Figured you might like to know."

Bowman shrugged carelessly, but his eyes were cold. "A man makes a livin' any way he can."

"Stillman pays good."

"Why not? It's mighty easy to spend someone else's money."

"I take it you don't cotton to Don Stillman."

"I'd feel easier around a rattlesnake."

Bowman tossed off the balance of his drink and set the glass carefully on the bar. "Jim, you've been followin' me around. Why?"

Kerby laughed. "You've got the wrong slant, Mace! I've got better things to do than follow anyone around."

Bowman said, "All right, Jim," nodded, and left the saloon, continuing his slow patrol of the town.

At ten Bowman dropped in at Jarrett's office, but the old doctor shook his head regretfully as the lawman entered.

"No change, Mace," he told him. "Get yourself some sleep, man! All this worryin' won't help the girl."

The lanky sheriff left the office, his spirits dampened. As he neared the gate he felt the cold, sharp blade of a knife pressed against the back of his neck, and he froze, muscles tensing against the expected thrust.

"*Señor* El Pardo wishes to see you," a man's low voice came from the darkness behind him. "Alive, if possible, but it's up to you, *Señor* Bowman."

The lawman recognized the voice of Carlos, the guard usually found at the gates of El Pardo's hacienda.

He said gruffly, "It's not El Pardo's way to summon his friends with the blade of a knife."

"Perhaps *Señor* El Pardo is not certain you are a friend," the *vaquero* retorted quickly. "Your horse is ready in the alley, *señor*. We will go."

Bowman caught sight of other shadowy figures in the darkness behind him as his six-gun was lifted from its holster. He considered but instantly rejected any thought of making a break for it, and under the none too gentle prodding of the knife, turned and walked toward the rear of the doctor's office. As he passed a lighted window he could see the scowling image of Carlos reflected barely a pace behind him, knife held low at his hip.

The *vaqueros* forced the pace as they left the town behind them, riding closely bunched around the lawman to prevent a sudden break into the mesquite. No words were spoken until the group reached the gates of the hacienda, and then only to identify the riders to the guards.

Once inside the gates, a heated argument developed between Carlos and a villainous-looking *vaquero* called Miguel. From the few words reaching the lawman's ears, it was apparent Carlos wished to take Bowman

to El Pardo at once, while Miguel, for some reason of
his own, indicated the stable with stabbing motions
of his arm. The two moved out of hearing as the quarrel continued, but Miguel seemed to make his point,
and the group moved off toward the stable. Carlos
ordered one of the *vaqueros* to see to the horses as they
entered a large, gloomy saddle room just off the corral.

The grim-visaged *vaquero* stepped in front of the
lawman, blocking his path. "*Señor* Bowman, you have
much to tell us. It would be best for all if you began
now, without delay."

Bowman asked bitingly, "Have you gone loco,
Carlos? You told me El Pardo wanted to see me.
Where is he?"

"In good time, *señor*," the *vaquero* replied, "when
you've told us what we must know."

"Talk sense, man!"

"*Señora* El Pardo and the *señorita*," Carlos persisted, "where are they?"

"Where would they be at this time of night except
at the hacienda?"

Carlos said swiftly, "They are not at the hacienda!
No one knows that better than you!"

Bowman shook his head. "You're not makin' any
sense, Carlos. Take me to El Pardo."

"I am responsible for what happened today," the *vaquero* said stiffly. "You will not see El Pardo until you tell us what you have done with the *señora* and the girl!"

Bowman said angrily, "I didn't do anything with them, you fool! I don't know what you're talkin' about."

Miguel leaped forward, brushing Carlos aside.

"Enough of this!" he roared. "Bete! Orlo!"

Two of the *vaqueros* ran forward and seized Bowman by the arms, dragging him toward the center of the room. The lawman let his weight sag between them, then suddenly braced his feet against the hard-packed earthen floor and hurled the two smaller men from him. Then the others came at him in a bunch, Miguel in the lead, and Bowman lashed out furiously with his big fists. He caught Miguel full in the face as he came charging in, and the force of the blow tumbled Miguel to the floor, blood spewing from broken lips. The others circled cautiously for a moment, wary of Bowman's punishing fists; then Miguel was on his feet, the long, thin, blade of the knife in his hand glittering menacingly in the flickering light of the lanterns.

"No!" Carlos shouted as he ran past the lawman and brought the edge of his hand in a slashing blow across the wrist of Miguel's knife hand. The Mexican dropped his knife and retreated a step, glaring fiercely at his attacker.

Carlos snarled, "You pig! El Pardo would quarter us all if the *señor* lawman suffered at our hands! Enough of this!"

Bowman took advantage of the momentary confusion to make a sudden break for the door. His hand was on the wooden latch when something crashed against the side of his head and tumbled him headlong to the floor. Black, swirling darkness clouded his eyes, and he was conscious neither of pain as he smashed helplessly into the rough planking of the door nor of rough hands which grasped him by the shoulders and dragged him back to the center of the room.

His head throbbed and his arms seemed as if they were being pulled from their sockets as the mists began to clear from his eyes. Ropes had been twisted about his wrists and thrown over a beam in the center of the room, and he found himself suspended in mid-air with the toes of his boots barely touching the floor. His shirt had been stripped from his back, and a bright sheen of sweat glistened on his bare shoulders.

Miguel, his face bloody from Bowman's slashing blows, stood a few feet away. Over the Mexican's shoulder Bowman could see Carlos with his shoulders braced against a far wall, *vaqueros* at his sides with knives held close to his chest.

Miguel followed the direction of his eyes. "Carlos is an old woman! Do not look to him for help, gringo!"

He walked to a post and pulled down a broad leather strap, drawing it gloatingly through his fingers.

"Now we will see what the gringo is made of!"

The snap of the leather across the bare muscles of his back sent rivers of pain spilling through Bowman's body. The strap rose and fell again, and with each vicious swing, Miguel called softly:

"Talk, you gringo dog!"

Time faded for Bowman as the strap slashed again and again across his back. Pain dimmed his senses until he scarcely felt the punishing leather, and he was only vaguely aware of the sudden shot which blasted out in the unnatural stillness of the room. As if in a dream, he saw Miguel stop in the midst of drawing his arm back for another blow, straighten slowly and allow the strap to slip through his lax fingers to the floor. He stood motionless for a moment, a look of surprise and disbelief on his face, then folded at the waist and crumpled face down on the floor.

The grim, cold face of Jim Kerby swam into Bowman's view. The ex-lawman stood near the door, waving a smoking six-gun in the faces of the stunned *vaqueros*.

"That bullet was aimed for his shoulder, but the next one will go in someone's heart! Cut Bowman down!"

Carlos snatched a knife from one of the *vaqueros* at his side and rushed to carry out the order. Kerby said harshly, "Help him!" and others steadied the lawman as Carlos slashed the ropes. Bowman, weaving drunkenly, brushed them away with a terse, "Get away from me!"

He steadied himself for a moment against the post, then reached down and picked up his shirt.

"Looks as if you got here in the nick of time, Jim, but how?"

"Over the wall," Kerby replied tersely. "Got a gun, Mace? Sounds like we're goin' to need all the powder we can burn."

Bowman could hear the swelling roar in the courtyard as Kerby slammed the door and dropped the heavy cross-bar into place. The shot had alerted the sleeping *vaqueros*, and apparently a hundred or more of them were rushing toward the saddle room. Carlos silently withdrew Bowman's six-gun from his belt and handed it over.

Someone was pounding on the door and shouting loudly in Spanish, "Open up or we'll break the door in!"

Kerby retreated to one side of the room and motioned Bowman to take up a post at the other.

"All right!" Kerby called. "Break it in! But some of you won't be goin' back to your sleepin' bags tonight if you do!"

From the subdued sounds just outside the door, the new arrivals were apparently having a hurried conference among themselves. Suddenly a new voice broke in, "What are you men doing here? Why is the door locked?"

Bowman exclaimed, "El Pardo!" and moved to the door, lifting the bar and swinging it wide. The slender Mexican stood framed in the doorway, shaking his head in bewilderment as his eyes rested first on the broad welts criss-crossing Mace Bowman's back and shoulders, then dropped to the motionless form of Miguel, and finally came to rest on the gate guard, Carlos.

"Carlos! You will explain this to me at once!"

Carlos, head hanging and eyes downcast, spoke rapidly in Spanish. When he had finished El Pardo said angrily, "You dog! You will answer to me for this outrage!"

"*Señor—*" Carlos began.

"I gave you certain duties," El Pardo said icily. "You have failed me!"

"Miguel—"

"I do not speak of Miguel! He is a jackal, and when he recovers from his wound, he will be banished from my hacienda!"

El Pardo turned to Bowman as several *vaqueros* hurried to the side of the faintly moaning Miguel. "You have my thanks for placing the bullet so carefully, *Señor* Bowman. You might have killed him just as easily."

Bowman jerked his thumb toward Jim Kerby. "You owe this gent your thanks; not me. If I'd had a gun in my hands when Miguel was layin' that strap across my back, I'd have put my first bullet right between his eyes!"

"You are a guest in my hacienda, and I am very sorry you were mistreated," El Pardo said a little stiffly. "I assure you the guilty ones will be severely punished. Now, if you please, there are other matters which must be discussed between us."

The walk to the main house was a silent one, each man seemingly deeply occupied with his own thoughts.

Once they were within the comfortable confines of the big living room, Bowman turned and caught El Pardo's eyes.

"We've been *amigos* for a long time, El Pardo," he said slowly. "Maybe you'd best tell me what this is all about."

The slender Mexican saw Bowman glance covertly at the open windows and said coldly, "There's is no escape, my friend. The hacienda is well guarded."

"I got over the walls without havin' to hurt anyone," Jim Kerby said pointedly. "After watchin' your boys manhandlin' Bowman, maybe I won't be so particular when I go out."

El Pardo's angry eyes locked with the ex-lawman's. "You are a brave man, my friend. The courtyard is swarming with a hundred *vaqueros* ready to tear you apart if I but give the signal."

"You'll be givin' it with the muzzle of my gun against your backbone!" Kerby said viciously.

Mace Bowman said hastily, "Jim—"

"Mace, I'm tired of listenin' to this fork-tongued, would-be badman!" Kerby interrupted angrily. "He's a big brave man with a hundred bloodthirsty cutthroats out there in the courtyard! He's mighty good at kidnappin' and floggin' and threatenin' to burn down the

homes of innocent women and children! But I'm wonderin' just how brave a man he is with the bore of a
.45 starin' him in the face."

Bowman held up his hand. "Jim, I've always known
Juan to be a brave man. Maybe we should listen to what
he has to say."

He turned to the Mexican. "It *is* strange that you
speak of escape, *amigo;* even stranger that you bring a
friend to your home at the point of a knife."

"These are troubled times, and it is not always easy
to tell friend from foe." He added tentatively, "You
have not delivered Don Stillman and his jackals to me."

"No, but that's not the reason you sent your *vaqueros*
after me," Bowman retorted. "They would have already told you Stillman is hidin' in the mesquite. I
can't do the impossible."

El Pardo asked suddenly, "Where are the *señorita*
and the *señora?*"

Bowman scowled, his patience wearing thin. "I'm
tired of that question! How should I know where they
are?"

The Mexican's dark, brooding eyes never left the
face of the lawman. "My mother and the *señorita* were
taken from the hacienda this morning, while I was
away on business. I have reason to believe you know

where they are!"

Bowman asked incredulously, "You left your women-folk unguarded?"

"No!" El Pardo snapped. "I left a number of *vaqueros* here, but the women were taken by trickery!"

He studied the lawman, making no effort to conceal the contempt in his eyes. "I believe you can tell me where they are."

Bowman said gruffly, "You believe wrong!"

El Pardo left his chair and placed a folded paper on the table beside the lawman. "You think El Pardo is a man of lies! Read your own words!"

Bowman unfolded the grimy, much handled paper and read its message in silence. *"El Pardo: We have your mother and your girl. You won't see them again if you raid Jurado."* It was signed, *"Mace Bowman."*

He handed it to Jim Kerby. "You figure I wrote this, Juan?"

"Did you not sign your name to it?"

"Who left this message?" Bowman asked curtly. "Who entered the gates of your hacienda and took your women-folk? Was it me, *amigo?*"

"Carlos described this jackal well," El Pardo said ominously. "It was the marshal of Jurado, Dave Thompson, and he said he was carrying a message from you."

Kerby asked harshly, "What fool let Thompson through the gate?"

"Why would your guards trust a man like Thompson," Bowman demanded, "knowin' he was the hombre who shot and killed Benavides?"

"The fault lies with me," El Pardo admitted glumly. "I failed to describe him to my guards and he did not identify himself when he approached the gates."

The lawman shook his head in disbelief. "You make mistakes like that and still hope to run Don Stillman out of the border country! Juan, you're like a puppy bracin' a timber wolf!"

The Mexican leader left his chair and paced slowly back and forth in front of the stone fireplace, his face lined with worry. The lawman said sharply, "Knowin' Thompson for what he is, would I be likely to send him out here?"

El Pardo remained silent, and Bowman took the murder warrant he was carrying for the Mexican's arrest from his pocket. He laid it on the table beside the note Thompson had left behind him.

"I didn't send Thompson out here," he said stolidly. "Take a look at the two signatures on these papers, *amigo*."

El Pardo carefully examined the two papers. He admitted finally, "They are not the same, Mace! But what can Thompson hope to gain by this trickery?"

"He's a mighty smart hombre," Bowman replied thoughtfully. "He knows if he can stop you from burnin' Jurado, he'll be a big man in the town. And he figures he can do it by threatenin' to kill your women-folk if you ride on Jurado."

He rubbed his jaw. "If that's his plan, some of the other things happenin' around here make sense, *amigo*, like the shootin' of Benavides and the disappearance of Nick Valdes. He knows that if he can keep you and Jurado riled up enough, sooner or later you're goin' to make a move that'll bring the army down on your neck. In the meantime, he'll be fillin' his pockets with all the plums."

El Pardo struck his clenched fist against the palm of his hand in anger. "Then he is a fool! My *vaqueros* will ride to Jurado tonight and take this jackal! He'll talk, *amigo*, believe me!"

The lawman shook his head in disagreement. "You'll never take Thompson alive, and he wouldn't talk if you did, Juan."

Jim Kerby agreed. "I know Thompson better than most men, El Pardo. He'll know his only chance is to keep your women-folk alive and where you can't find them. Nothin' you can do to him will change that."

"Carlos will make him talk," El Pardo said confidently. "Such men have ways with their enemies, my friends. Death is sometimes easier."

"But if he doesn't talk?" Bowman asked pointedly. "If he dies first? Your mother and the *señorita* would die with him, Juan, of thirst, or hunger, or even worse."

El Pardo said in a low voice filled with hate, "They cannot remain in his hands!"

"He won't harm them unless you force his hand," Kerby said with conviction.

El Pardo slumped dejectedly into a chair. "I have been defeated by my own carelessness!"

"You were a fool to give Thompson a chance to pull a stunt like this," Bowman agreed bluntly. "But it's too late for back-trackin' now. We've got to figure out a way to get the women away from him before we move in."

Kerby said, "There's a chance Thompson will give himself away if he figures Bowman doesn't know anything about this. Not much of a chance, but about the only one we have."

"I could send my *vaqueros* out into the mesquite," El Pardo said thoughtfully, "and have them search every inch of ground between here and Jurado. It is possible they could find his hiding place."

"A waste of time, *amigo*," Bowman returned. "They might search for weeks and never come within a mile of where he has your women. And if your *vaqueros* are ridin' all over the range, Thompson might let the women die rather than take a chance on tryin' to reach them."

"Sit tight," Kerby advised. "Let Thompson make a mistake, if he's goin' to."

"But how long must we do nothing?"

Bowman considered. "It might take a week, even longer. Who can tell?"

El Pardo made his decision, and his face was grim. "Until Sunday, at dawn. No longer. If my mother and the *señorita* have not been returned to me by then, Jurado will celebrate the Sabbath in a bath of flames!"

"Until Sunday," Bowman agreed. He rose from his chair and flexed his shoulders, grimacing with pain. El Pardo noticed the grimace.

"Carlos exceeded his authority," he said. "Suitable punishment will be meted out."

"Forget it," Bowman replied gruffly. "Carlos did what he thought he had to."

Their horses were waiting for them near the big

gates, and soon they were riding rapidly along the trail toward Jurado. Bowman said thoughtfully, "I can't figure your stake in this, Jim. Thought you were were workin' for Stillman."

"He don't own me," Kerby replied gruffly, and the rest of the ride was made in silence.

## Seven

Early the following morning, Mace Bowman left his room and made his way down to the lobby of the hotel. His face was lined with weariness, the few hours of restless sleep having done little to ease the tension of his taut nerves. The respite reluctantly granted by Juan El Pardo gave Jurado a few more days of grace but left the town's future as bleak as ever. Bowman was certain the proud Mexican had no intention of forgoing his plans for leveling the border town, even if the kidnapped women were found within the allotted time. El Pardo's blood vengeance against Don Stillman had not and would not be forgotten.

Bowman reluctantly left the relative coolness of the lobby behind him and moved out into the street, blinking his eyes against the already merciless sun. Heat waves boiled from the boardwalk and from the weather-bleached boards of every building. Dust devils were born and died as he watched, and gradually fading clouds of dust particles relentlessly followed all who ventured out into the street. He walked along in his awkward and ambling gait, moving the grit in his mouth with the tip of his tongue, spitting and finding it still there and knowing it always would be as long as he remained in the parched border country.

Doc Jarrett glanced up as Bowman pushed through the door, and nodded a brief greeting.

"Reckon I'll have to start charging you room rent," he grunted amiably, "or have the town dock your pay for all the time you spend here when you're supposed to be out protecting the honest folks of Jurado." He added dryly, "If there are any honest people in Jurado."

The lawman asked, "How is Lucy?"

"Came out of the coma this morning," Jarrett told him. "She still has a high fever, but if I can break it soon enough, I think she'll have a good chance of making it."

"Any chance of seein' her?"

Jarrett hesitated for a moment, then nodded. "Maybe for a few minutes, Mace. Don't excite her, and remember she may not recognize you, what with the fever and shock."

But Lucy did recognize him as he approached the side of her bed. She exclaimed weakly, "Mace!"

Her face was lined with pain and flushed with fever, but she managed a faint smile. Bowman reached out for her hand and pressed it gently between his own.

"Doc says you'll be up before you know it!"

She asked, "What happened?"

"I reckon you stopped a bullet meant for me, Lucy."

She raised her head a few inches from the pillow. "Who was it, Mace? Who would want to kill you?"

He laughed dryly. "I could think of a dozen or more without any trouble!"

"Don Stillman?"

"Maybe," he evaded.

Her head dropped back on the pillow and she closed her eyes wearily. Bowman leaned over and awkwardly placed a kiss on her forehead.

"Get well soon, Lucy," he whispered. "We can't keep the padre waitin'!"

Her eyes remained closed, but a faint smile curled the corners of her lips. "Padre?"

"I've been meanin' to ask you to marry me," he confessed, red-faced. "Maybe this isn't exactly the right time, but—"

Bowman didn't finish the sentence. Lucy had fallen asleep with the smile still on her lips and the lawman retreated from the room.

"Take good care of your patient, Doc," he warned good-naturedly, "or I'll personally see to it that you enjoy a stay at my hotel!"

The crusty old doctor snorted his derision. "You're like a toothless old wolf howling at the moon, Mace! Not many folks you can frighten any more, except babies and old maids, and only those because you're so doggone ugly!"

Bowman grinned and left the office, heartened by even the small progress Lucy had made. Entering the small restaurant beside the hotel, he saw Don Stillman and Virgil Storey already seated at one of the tables. Stillman motioned for him to join them.

"Never expected to see you gents in town," the lawman said curtly, dropping into a chair. "Not as long as El Pardo is on the loose."

He signaled for coffee. "Where are your pards?"

"Here in town, where they have every right to be," Stillman snapped. "We're back because the man we hired to do a job is doing it! Can't say as much for you, Bowman."

The lawman ignored the thrust. "Thompson kill El

Pardo?"

"There's other ways of keepin' that outlaw in hand," Storey interjected.

"Maybe," the lawman agreed politely. "Just what would they be, Storey?"

"I don't see it as any of your business!" the rancher snapped. "But when the elections come up again, keep in mind Dave Thompson is doin' the job you're bein' paid for!"

Bowman took a long drink of the bitter black coffee. Through the window he saw Denver Rogers ride up and drop his reins over the hitching rail in front of the eating place. The stocky deputy came through the open door and made his way directly to the table where the three men sat.

"They turned me back, Mace!" he said ruefully, dropping wearily into a chair. Bowman motioned for more coffee. "El Pardo has this neck of the woods roped in tight as a ringed bull! Polite as the devil about it, but his *vaqueros* make it plenty clear no one is ridin' through to the outside."

Stillman broke in, "What's this all about?"

"Denver was ridin' north to the army post," Bowman returned curtly. "He didn't make it."

He turned to Virgil Storey. "Seen your range boss

yet? El Pardo cleaned you out yesterday, rustlin' every steer that could walk. Then he put the torch to your buildin's and stacks."

The rancher leaped to his feet, upsetting his coffee over the table. "The devil you say!"

"It's only the beginnin'," Bowman pointed out. "It's my guess he'll clean out every spread you gents stole from the Mexicans."

Stillman swore feelingly. "Not without a fight he won't! I'll get the army here pronto!"

The lawman asked, "How? You heard what Denver said."

Storey muttered, "There's got to be a way out."

"Denver, maybe you could ride south across the river, then circle around behind El Pardo's *vaqueros*," Bowman suggested.

"It's worth a try," the deputy agreed instantly.

"Hold off until dark," the lawman said. "Might give you a better chance of gettin' through."

The deputy nodded and left. Bowman turned to Don Stillman.

"You jaspers are loco if you figure on stayin' here in Jurado. The folks here are all in favor of turnin' you over to El Pardo, and the sooner the better, they figure. You've no friends here, Stillman."

"It's your job to protect us."

"It's the marshal's job. You made it clear enough that Thompson was takin' over Jurado."

He left the two glowering furiously and picked up his horse at the livery stable, riding south toward the river. He faced a blank wall in the kidnapping of the two women. There was only the slim chance that Thompson might be concealing them in one of the abandoned cabins along the river, and the even slimmer chance that he could find it in time to stop El Pardo from sacking Jurado.

Reaching the river and swinging to the west, he rode for more than an hour without finding anything to arouse his suspicions. He passed a score of deserted shacks, but none showed any signs of recent occupation.

As he rode out of a thick clump of mesquite, Bowman's horse almost trampled the prone form of the Reverend Jack Benteen, who was stretched out in the shade of a tree on the river bank, snoring lustily. One end of a long fishing pole was stuck in the mud of the bank, and the other vibrated vigorously.

Bowman dismounted, pulled in the line and discovered that the padre had unwittingly hooked a good-size catfish. Dutifully he baited the hook from a can near the sleeper's outstretched hand and cast the line back into the river. Jack Benteen still snored with great gusto.

The lanky sheriff debated whether or not to wake the sleeping padre, and finally decided against it. He was about to swing back into the saddle when he stopped, suddenly suspicious.

Benteen said politely, "Thank you, Mace! I always did hate to bait a hook, you know. Nice fish you have there, too."

Bowman turned. The padre was still stretched out comfortably, but he was smiling, his head cradled on his forearm. The lawman laughed ruefully.

"Well, Padre, you were snoring like you meant it," he said good-naturedly. "Hate to bother a man that busy!"

"The snoring was purely for effect," Benteen assured him. "Actually I was thinking about my next sermon when you rode up. What brings you down here, Mace?"

Bowman related the details of the kidnapping and his futile search for the two women, certain the information would go no farther than the padre's ears. Benteen sobered at once.

"It's a terrible thing, Mace," he said in a low voice. "Only the Lord knows what Thompson may have done to those poor folks by now."

"They're alive, at least," the lawman guessed. "They'd be no good to Thomspon dead."

Benteen pulled in his line and concealed the pole in the thick grass at the edge of the river. "I'll ride with you, Mace."

Bowman nodded his thanks. As they rode out of the small clearing, the padre held up his hand. "May not mean a thing, but there's a deserted shack about a mile east of here, a bit back from the river. I rode past it on my way down and noticed a horse tied behind it."

The lawman, eager for any lead, wheeled his horse. "Let's go!"

They found the ramshackle cabin without difficulty, one of many along the river, despite the fact that it was almost completely concealed in a heavy mesquite thicket. They dismounted in a heavy mesquite stand and cautiously worked their way forward, keeping low in the thick cover. Bowman held up his hand when they reached a spot on the edge of the small clearing in which the shack rested.

"You're not packin' a gun, Padre, so stay under-cover," he said in a low voice. "Come up when I give the signal."

He covered half the distance to the cabin in a

crouching run before dropping behind the shelter of a
rotten log, but no shots were fired. On his feet again
quickly, he raced for the rotting timbers of the porch,
hugging the wall beside the open door. Still no sound
came from inside the crumbling shack.

Raising his voice, he called, "We have you boxed
in, gents! Come out with your hands over your heads!"

Silence followed his words. He risked a quick glance
past the edge of his shelter, then straightened slowly
and sheathed his gun. With a wave of his hand he signaled for Jack Benteen to come up.

The padre glanced over Bowman's shoulder and said
softly, "May God have mercy on his soul!"

The sheriff slipped a knife from his belt and moved
into the room, Benteen following at his heels. Reaching
up, he slashed the rope and eased the limp body of a
man to the littered floor of the shack.

He said in a low voice, "Now we know what happened to Nick Valdes."

The padre asked, "El Pardo?"

"Someone wants us to think so," Bowman returned
grimly. "But this isn't El Pardo's work. If he was
fixin' to hang one of Stillman's bunch, he'd do it right
in the center of Jurado."

"It may have been Dave Thompson."

"Maybe," the sheriff replied noncommittally. "I reckon he's the only one who fits into this thing, but I'm not sure exactly how."

He released a deep breath. "Thompson's a mighty ambitious man and a rough one. But one thing stumps me, Padre. Nick Valdes disappeared three days ago, but I figure he hasn't been dead more than an hour!"

He moved toward the door. "Nothin' more we can do here, Padre. I'll get the horses."

He was framed in the doorway when a shot splintered the sun-dried wood near his head. He dropped quickly to the floor and rolled back into the protection of the shack as Benteen ran to one of the paneless windows and crouched down beside it.

"Watch yourself, Padre!" Bowman called. "That gent is usin' a rifle."

"Caught a glimpse of a bay over on the left," Benteen said in a low voice. "White stocking on its right hind leg. There it is! Beyond the cottonwood!"

"I saw it," Bowman returned, climbing to his feet. "He's lightin' out of here, whoever he is."

He moved swiftly through the door into the bright sunlight, crouching low, but no shots came. When he returned with the horses, Beenteen said, "That hombre didn't try very hard. He might've kept us pinned down here until dark."

"Hit and run," Bowman said briefly. "A drygulcher stays alive longer that way."

"Think it was Thompson?"

"He rides a bay with a white stocking on its right hind leg, but so does Jim Kerby."

In Jurado, Jack Benteen took the body of the slain rancher to the combination general store and undertaking parlor, and Bowman rode on to his office. There he found Don Stillman and his partners securely locked behind bars. Sandy Morgan was at the desk, and Gil Sheldon and a dozen others were scattered about the room.

Morgan spread his hands in a futile gesture when he saw the question in Bowman's eyes.

"Sheldon and his bunch brought them in," he explained. "Figured I'd better play along with them until you got back."

The sheriff nodded, turning to Sheldon who appeared to be the leader of the group. "Give me the story, Gil."

"We made a citizen's arrest of Stillman and the others," Sheldon said promptly. "Nothin' illegal about that, Mace. We figure to give them a fair trial, then turn them over to El Pardo."

"Fair trial?" Bowman asked, sarcasm heavy in his

voice. "You've got them convicted already!"

Sheldon returned coolly, "Why not, Sheriff? We all know they're guilty!"

"Of what?"

"Thievery, murder, assault and anything else you might mention," the other told him. "Plus puttin' the folks of Jurado in danger of their lives by what they've done to the Mexicans."

"Murphy goin' to try the case?"

"That crooked jasper will be lucky if we don't put him on trial, too!" Sheldon retorted. "He's as big a crook as Stillman and the others; maybe bigger. It's our intention to appoint a judge to try those hombres, Mace."

"Won't be legal," Bowman said. "You may find yourself answerin' to the soldiers for it."

"We'll worry about that when the time comes!"

"How about Dave Thompson?" the lawman asked. "El Pardo wants him as bad as he does the others."

"We figure he'll be satisfied without Thompson."

Bowman rubbed the side of his jaw thoughtfully. "When's this trial takin' place?"

"Tonight, at the Maverick. By that time we may have Nick Valdes in a cell with the others."

Bowman said evenly, "You might just meet up with

him at that, Gil, but not in Jurado."

He turned toward the door, and Sheldon called after him, "Like to have you there, Sheriff. Make it a mite more legal."

Bowman said nothing as he stepped out on the boardwalk. Sandy Morgan hurried after him.

"What do you want me to do, Mace?"

"Stay in there and keep an eye on things," Bowman instructed. "It's about all you can do, Sandy."

Morgan looked puzzled. "You goin' to let Sheldon get away with this?"

Bowman said tersely, "Son, those hombres are a lot safer in a cell than they would be walkin' the streets of Jurado. Take my word for it."

The blind Manuel Hernandez called out a cheery greeting as he approached the Maverick, and Bowman replied absently.

Inside the saloon, Collins placed a bottle and glass in front of him.

"Got new law in Jurado," the bartender said, jerking his head at the table where Gil Sheldon and several others sat.

Bowman said nothing, tossing off his drink and pouring another. Maxine came up and stood silently at his elbow.

"Mace—" the girl began, then looked over the sheriff's shoulder and saw Dave Thompson approaching. A look of fear passed over her face.

"Hello, Maxine. Howdy, Sheriff," the gunman greeted them as he came up. Bowman grunted but said nothing.

"I hear some of the boys are puttin' on a trial in here tonight," Thompson mentioned. "Reckon you're goin' to break it up, Sheriff?"

Bowman said shortly, "No."

"It's a drumhead court," the gunman reasoned. "Not legal."

"Lots of things might seem legal when you're lookin' down the barrel of a six-gun."

Thompson threatened, "If you don't break it up, I will!"

"It's your town. Only be mighty careful how you use that iron of yours."

Without a word Thompson took the girl's arm, and the two walked toward the far end of the bar. Shrugging, Mace picked up the bottle and glass and wandered to a table in a corner, taking a position where he could watch both front and back entrances.

The lawman drank steadily, but his eyes remained clear and alert. Darkness fell and the curious began drifting into the saloon, men and women alike, the news of the forthcoming trial proving an irresistible attraction. The fearful tension gripping the small town seemed to have lessened, and the interior of the saloon was a scene of boisterous gayety. Not even the appearance of the defendants, shackled and heavily guarded, dampened the high spirits of the crowd.

Under Gil Sheldon's direction, tables and chairs were quickly dragged into position near the back of the room, and twelve men Bowman guessed to be the jury took their places at one side. Sheldon then climbed to a chair and shouted for attention.

"I reckon you all know why we're here," he said importantly, "so we might as well get right down to business. I've been elected to act as judge, and those hombres over there will be the jury. Stillman and his pards are bein' tried for crimes endangerin' the safety of Jurado, and if they're found guilty, we intend turnin' them over to El Pardo!"

Someone came up and took a chair beside Bowman, and he bobbed his head in a greeting.

"Thought you might be along, Padre."

Sheldon was speaking again. "Any of you hombres who want to testify, come right on up! We don't want any doubt that this is a fair trial."

He climbed down from the chair and took his seat behind a whiskey-stained table, rapping for order with the butt of his six-gun.

"Court is now in session!"

Jack Benteen said mildly, "I see it's your intention to allow this trial to continue."

"It's their town," Bowman shrugged. "I reckon no one blames them for doin' what they think they have to."

"We have a legal court of law in Jurado."

Bowman laughed without humor. "Same as Stillman judgin' himself if you put Murphy behind that table."

Dave Thompson watched the proceedings from a position near the railing of the balcony, a contemptuous smile on his lips. It was not his intention to allow the hastily contrived trial to reach its conclusion, but for the moment he was content to stand back and observe. He experienced no qualms about the fairness of the trial or its legality, but his own purposes would be served best by keeping Stillman alive for a few more days.

He slid his six-gun from his holster and, aiming carefully, triggered it twice in rapid succession, both bullets burying themselves in the table inches from Gil Sheldon's hand. A giant wave of silence washed over the big room in the wake of the booming reports.

The gunman called loudly, "The next bullet might be in someone's head! Sheldon, climb out of that chair and turn those gents loose."

Gil Sheldon leaped to his feet, his face working with fury. "You fool! This crowd will tear you to pieces!"

"Maybe," the gunman conceded coolly, "but not before a few of them are stretched out in the sawdust! Now turn those hombres loose!"

The infuriated Sheldon, his natural caution tempered by the raw whiskey he had consumed, made a desperate grab for the six-gun on the table in front of him. Thompson's next shot sent the weapon skidding from the table.

The gunman's voice was deadly when he spoke again from the balcony. "Sheldon, you're a dead man if you go after that gun!"

A rider at a table next to Bowman's stealthily began easing his gun from its holster. The lawman reached out and brought the edge of his hand sharply across the other's wrist, and the surprised cowboy gave a grunt of pain.

Bowman asked caustically, "You want a fast ride to Boot Hill?"

The gunman called, "I'll tell you once more! Sheldon, turn those gents loose!"

Sheldon produced a key and quickly unlocked the shackles binding the prisoners. On the balcony, Thompson waved his gun threateningly.

"Now you hombres clear out of here!" he ordered sharply. "And chew this over. "I'll hang the first jasper who tries a stunt like this in my town again!"

The smoke-clouded room gradually cleared of all but a few of the more determined. The five ex-prisoners, laughing and joking among themselves, moved up to the bar and motioned for Thompson to join them, but the hard-eyed gunman shook his head and disappeared into one of the rooms behind him.

Jack Benteen looked inquiringly at the sheriff, but Bowman shook his head. "Sheldon is lucky to be alive, Padre. I don't reckon he'll bring any charges against Thompson."

Benteen asked thoughtfully, "What made him think he could buck a man like Thompson?"

"Whiskey," Bowman said tersely. "Boot Hill is full of gents with the same kind of sand."

He pushed back his chair and climbed to his feet. "Let's get out of here, Padre. There's things needin' to be done."

## Eight

Jack Benteen sat behind a small table in the converted saloon he and his small congregation used as a makeshift church. Evidence of the building's former status in the community could easily be seen in the long bar, the cracked and broken mirrors and the many rough, whiskey-stained tables stacked up at one end of the room.

The lamp on the table, turned low, flickered and smoked as the front door was steathily opened and closed, but if the padre noticed he gave no sign. Although it was nearing midnight, writing materials were spread haphazardly on the table, and the pen in Benteen's big fingers moved laboriously across the sheet of paper in front of him.

The two shadowy figures, moving cautiously through the scattered chairs, stopped twenty feet from the table where Benteen sat, just beyond the circle of yellow light cast by the lamp.

Without looking up, Benteen asked, "Is there something I can do for you?"

"Yeah," a voice drawled from the shadows. "You can die."

From the open back door of the church Jim Kerby shouted, "Get down, Padre!" and the two quick shots he triggered sounded almost as one. A swarm of bullets smashed into the wall behind him as he plunged in a headlong dive to the floor, rolling. He triggered another shot, this time at the lamp, and the big room was suddenly plunged into darkness. More bullets, aimed at the muzzle flash of his gun, searched for him in the darkness, but he was moving and the shots were wide of the mark. A rush of stumbling feet sounded near the back door; there was the crash of a falling chair, then silence.

Mace Bowman, just leaving the sheriff's office, heard the shots and raced for the church. When he reached it moments later, Jim Kerby had found another lamp to replace the one shattered by his bullet, and was standing silently by the still form of Jack Benteen. When Bowman reached his side, Kerby pointed at the ominous black hole just over the right temple of the padre.

He said soberly, "I tried to help him, but I got here too late."

Bowman knew by the position of the wound that nothing could be done for Jack Benteen. Steely-eyed, he swung to face Jim Kerby.

"What are you doin' here, Jim?"

"I was walkin' past the church when I saw two men inside with the padre. Both of them had guns in their hands. I ran around to the back and tried to pot them, but I reckon I missed. I shot the lamp out, and in the confusion they both got away through the back door. When I found another lamp I saw the padre stretched out on the floor. That's about all, Mace."

"What did those two hombres look like?"

"I just saw their outlines against the lamp, Mace. Too dark to get a good look at their faces."

Sandy Morgan came running up, shock spreading over his face when he saw the still form of the padre. He asked almost in a whisper, "Who did this, Mace?"

Bowman shook his head. "I don't know, Sandy. But I'll find out, and when I do—"

His cold eyes and grim features finished the sentence for him. Morgan said, "Tell me what I can do, Mace."

"Look up Don Stillman," Bowman replied grimly. "You'll probably find him at the Border Hotel. Throw him in a cell and keep him there until I tell you different."

He swung to face Jim Kerby. "You're workin' for Stillman, Jim. Any objections to what I just told Sandy"

"You're the law in this town, Mace," Kerby said mildly. "Stillman doesn't pay me to keep him out of jail."

"Just what *does* he pay you for?"

Kerby shrugged. "For bein' around when he needs me, I reckon."

Morgan left, and Bowman said, "Stay with the padre until Doc Jarrett gets here, Jim. And don't ride out of town. I may want to talk to you again about this."

Bowman left the church and moved along the darkened street until he reached the Maverick. Manuel Hernandez, the blind *vaquero*, was there in his accustomed place, his sightless eyes staring off in the darkness. When he heard the lawman's footsteps, he said politely, "Good evening, *Señor* Bowman."

"Howdy, Manuel," Bowman replied, toeing a chair close to the blind man and dropping heavily into it.

He said glumly, "We've lost a good friend tonight."

The Mexican nodded. "We will miss the padre."

"He gave a little of himself to each of us," the sheriff murmured, "and asked nothin' in return."

"Who gives the eagle crumbs?" the blind man returned. "The padre needed nothing from us, *Señor* Bowman. He had his God and his work."

"He needs something from us now, Manuel," Bowman said in a strained voice. "Help to punish the jaspers who shot him down."

Manuel shook his head slowly.

"Benteen was a man of God," he countered. "His slaying will not go unavenged."

"Maybe God would appreciate a little help," Bowman suggested.

The *vaquero* said nothing, and Bowman asked suddenly, "Who killed the padre, Manuel?"

Manuel spread his hands, palms up. "I am blind, my friend. How could I know these things?"

Bowman leaned back in his chair, closing his eyes.

"When your wife took sick last year," he mused, "it was the padre who brought food and medicine and so eased the pain of her last few days."

"He was a good man," the Mexican agreed. "We will miss him."

Bowman said again, a sharp note in his voice, "Who was it, Manuel?"

The blind *vaquero* moved restlessly in his chair.

"Santos and Payne," he said. The words barely reached Bowman's ears. He climbed to his feet, kicking the chair back against the wall of the saloon.

*"Gracias, amigo!"*

"South and a little east," the blind man said quietly, as if talking to himself. "A cabin, near the banks of the river."

Bowman repeated, *"Gracias,"* and hurried along the street toward the livery stable. Moments later he was in the saddle and heeling his mount south under the brilliant light of a full moon.

When he reached the cabin, he found it shrouded in darkness. Dismounting, he circled the ramshackle building but found nothing to indicate that it was occupied. Reasoning that the two men he sought had not yet returned from Jurado, he concealed his mount in a mesquite thicket and started across the clearing.

He was no more than three steps from the protective mesquite when deadly orange-colored fingers of flame lanced out toward him from both front windows of the shack and the thunderous sound of gunfire beat out upon the quiet of the night. Bullets snapped past his head and tugged at his hat and clothing even as he dived desperately for the shelter of the mesquite. He rolled over, and the lethal leaden pellets followed his path, always close but never quite finding their target. Then he was in the mesquite, stretched on his back, his breath coming in great gasps and sweat oozing from every pore of his body.

Finally he rolled to his knees behind the trunk of a tree and opened fire on the shack. Instantly a swarm of bullets sought out his hiding place, and he retreated quickly to a new position. Time seemed to stand still as he streamed a hail of lead through the open windows, moved, fired, moved again. Each time the gunmen barricaded behind the walls of the shack returned the fire, shooting quickly but not too accurately at the muzzle flashes of his six-gun. From the sustained gunfire they were able to direct at him, Bowman knew there were at least four men in the dark confines of the cabin, possibly more.

It was not until he heard the snort of a horse far to his left that Bowman realized that no answering shots had come from the cabin for some time. He fired a tentative shot, then another, but the windows of the shack remained dark and soundless. Then the sound of racing horses came to him, and he leaped to his feet, running for his own mount. The ambushers, he thought angrily, had merely slipped from the cabin through a back window or door while he poured shot after shot into an empty room.

By the time Bowman reached his horse, the night was once again quiet, and he knew it would be hopeless to try to pick up the trail of the gunmen in the darkness. He returned to the cabin and searched it carefully, but found nothing but bullet-shattered utensils and furniture. A moment later he was back in the saddle, headed for Jurado, more than a little puzzled by the unexpectedness of the ambush. Apparently Benteen's killers had known he would follow them, and he set up a trap to do away with him once and for all. But how had they known he would be there at that particular time?

Less than a mile from the shack where the ambush had been staged, a sudden movement in the mesquite to his right attracted his attention, and he reined in sharply. Holding his horse motionless, his eyes probed the shadows for several moments without success. Then, as he was about to heel his mount forward, the brief movement came again, and this time Bowman saw the cause of it.

Two horses were tethered in a mesquite thicket only a few yards away, and barely visible in the uncertain light was the dark, squat shape of a cabin. No lights showed in the windows as Bowman swung quickly to the ground, and no alarm was sounded. He edged close to the nervous animals and searched their flanks for brands.

A moment was all he needed; then his lips tightened and he slowly backed away.

Dave Thompson was at the Maverick when the news of the shooting of Jack Benteen and the subsequent arrest of Don Stillman reached him. He waited in the shadows of the alley next to the saloon until he saw Mace Bowman ride out, then hurried to the jail. Sandy Morgan was at the desk, and the gunman nodded curtly as he passed on his way to the cell where Stillman nervously paced back and forth.

The land speculator said urgently, "Get me out of here, Dave!"

Morgan called, "If you're figurin' on lettin' that coyote go, forget it! Mace took the keys with him."

The gunman ignored him. "Bowman have anything on you, Don?"

"Not a thing!" Stillman replied confidently.

"I reckon maybe he has," Thompson said slyly. "I saw him talkin' to the blind *vaquero* in front of the Maverick; then he lit out toward the river."

"No concern of mine," Stillman replied, attempting to put indifference into his voice but failing.

"Might be, if the sheriff catches up with Santos and Payne."

"I don't know what you're talking about!" the land speculator retorted. "All I want is to get out of here!"

"Maybe you'll have to stay for a spell." Thompson grinned. "You heard what the deputy said."

"Shoot the lock off the door!"

"Can't do that, Don. I'm paid to uphold the law, not bust it."

"You're paid to do as I tell you!"

"Not any more, Don! Not any more."

Stillman gripped the bars of his cell until the knuckles of his fingers showed white.

"See Judge Murphy," he urged. "He'll issue an order for my release."

"Murphy can't do anything for you, but maybe I can."

"That's what I'm paying you for!"

"I reckon you're not paying me enough, Don."

Stillman said in a dangerously calm voice, "Just what *is* your price, Thompson?"

"Half of everything you own," the gunman replied calmly.

"For what?" Stillman shouted angrily.

"For your life," Thompson returned coolly.

"I'll rot in jail first!"

"You won't rot in jail," the gunman assured him. "I figure you'll hang. And pronto."

Stillman laughed harshly. "Not on any evidence Bowman can dig up against me!"

Thompson grinned. "If it comes to that, he'll have all the evidence he needs, Don. I'll see to it personally."

Stillman's face blanched. His eyes locked with those of the gunman, and in their cold, ruthless depths he saw the truth of his spoken words. Thompson would see him hang, if he had to fabricate the evidence to send him to the scaffold. He had no choice but to agree to the gunman's terms now, but when the time came—

He nodded curtly. "I figure my life is worth that much, Thompson. Now get me out of here."

"Not as easy as that, Don. I'll have Murphy draw up some papers makin' me your full partner; then we'll talk about gettin' you out of here."

He turned away and headed for the street.

"The way your pards are gettin' themselves knocked off, *partner*, maybe you're safer where you are!" he said over his shoulder. Behind him the land speculator smiled a secret smile of his own, as if silently enjoying a particularly amusing joke.

Mace Bowman rode into Jurado just before dawn

and went directly to his room at the Border Hotel. He touched a match to the wick of a lamp near the door, and a voice behind him said, "Hello, Mace! I've been waiting for you."

Bowman spun on his heel, his face going white.

"Padre!" he exclaimed incredulously. "I thought you were dead!"

## Nine

Bowman groaned, twisting over on his stomach and burying his head in his arms to quiet the incessant pounding. Except for boots and hat, he was fully dressed. After the padre had left early that morning, he had kicked off his boots, sprawled on the bed and dropped immediately into a deep, dreamless sleep.

Half asleep, he recalled vividly his own astonishment at discovering a supposedly dead man sitting calmly in a chair and grinning across the room at him. A small white bandage near his right temple gleamed starkly against the sun-darkened skin of his forehead, but otherwise Benteen seemed to have suffered no ill effects from the attempt upon his life.

"I guess I came as close to dying as a man could and still stay alive." The padre had smiled. "Doc Jarrett said the force of the bullet had spent itself before it struck me in the temple. Made a nasty hole and gave me quite a headache, but that's about all. Doc said something about defective powder or a poor loading job."

Mace had dropped wearily on the edge of the bed. "Do me a favor, Padre. Get lost for a few days. I've got enough to worry about without havin' to wonder who's goin' to take the next crack at you."

Benteen had left his chair and moved toward the door. "All right, Mace. I guess a little fishing trip wouldn't do me any harm."

The pounding continued, loud and persistent. Bowman rolled over, dropping his feet to the floor and cursing silently. He called, "I'm comin'!" in a rasping voice as he fumbled for his boots. His head ached and his body was stiff from countless hours in the saddle; he felt as if only a moment had passed since he had dropped, exhausted, on the bed. But the dusty rays of the late morning sun, etching a familiar pattern on the floor of the room, told him the day was already almost half gone.

He shouted, "Who is it?" as he strapped on his six-gun and moved toward the door.

"It's me, Morgan!" the excited voice of the young deputy called.

Bowman swung the door open and stepped aside, motioning for the deputy to enter. He asked sourly, "Don't you young hellions reckon I need any sleep?"

"I thought you ought to know about this, Mace," Morgan said, a note of apology in his voice. "Old Able Ferguson stumbled across a body this mornin' in the alley beside the Maverick. One of the dance hall girls."

Sleep was forgotten. "Which one?"

"The pretty one they call Maxine," Morgan told him. "The girl Dave Thompson was makin' a big play for."

Bowman said tersely, "Let's go!"

The girl's body lay against the outside wall of the Maverick, like a broken and useless doll cast aside by some giant hand. The narrow alley, littered with bottles and the rotting debris accumulated over the years, was already crowded with the curious.

Bowman shoved his way through the tightly packed mass, Sandy Morgan close at his heels. Someone had mercifully thrown a blanket over the still form of the girl, and the lawman dropped to one knee, peeling the covering back with a sweep of his arm. The girl's head was twisted unnaturally to one side, and Bowman guessed she had died of a broken neck.

"Looks like she fell or was pushed out of that window," Morgan said.

Bowman looked up. On the second floor of the

saloon, almost directly over the girl's body, a frayed and torn lace curtain hung half in and half out an open window. By its location, the sheriff knew it was one of several in the room occupied by the girl. He dropped the blanket in place and climbed to his feet. He said vehemently, "Clear out!" and the crowd, muttering sullenly, began to move back.

Jim Kerby pushed his way to Bowman's side. He said in a low, strained voice, "It's Maxine!"

The gaunt sheriff nodded, quickly fastening his hand on Kerby's arm as he tried to step past. The ex-lawman jerked free and bent, lifting the blanket but allowing it to drop back in place almost at once. His face was bleak with suppressed rage when he turned to Bowman.

"Dave Thompson!"

"We don't know that, Jim," Bowman said reasonably. "It might have been an accident. But if you know anything about this, you'd best tell me now. Don't make it a private war of your own."

Kerby moved around the lawman and headed for the street, blindly shoving stragglers from his path. Near the mouth of the alley, Mary Pearson came up to him and spoke softly, but Kerby either did not hear, or would not. He walked past the girl without a word, disappearing around a corner of the Maverick, leaving her staring after him with puzzled eyes.

Bowman arranged for the removal of the girl's body and walked slowly out to the street. For the first time he noticed the unusual number of *vaqueros* moving silently about the town. While most of them were strangers to him, he recalled seeing several of them recently at the hacienda of Juan El Pardo. Glancing down the street, he saw the slender Mexican leader leaning against a post on the veranda of the Border Hotel.

He murmured "Ah!" and directed his steps along the boardwalk toward the hotel.

Across the street, Dave Thompson pulled his horse to a sudden stop in the shadows of the livery stable, instantly suspicious of the large number of heavily armed *vaqueros* moving about. He knew instinctively that these were the men of Juan El Pardo, and he also knew that the slender Mexican would like nothing better than to lay his hands on the killer of Rafael Benavides.

The gunman was returning to Jurado from an early morning trip to the old cabin where he was holding *Señora* El Pardo and Marguerita Cardenas prisoners. When he had ridden into the small clearing, he had been thunderstruck to find nothing but charred ruins where the shack had once stood. The horses, left tethered at the rear of the building, were gone, and he assumed they had broken loose when the fire started. He had found no trace of his two prisoners and believed both had died in the blaze, roped tightly in the bunks where he had left them.

Back in Jurado, he slowly and carefully edged his mount closer to the street, keeping well within the shadows cast by the walls of the stable. The strange *vaqueros* worried him more than a little; he had not anticipated their presence in town and he needed time to adjust his plans accordingly. Across the street Mace Bowman climbed the steps to the veranda of the hotel, and a slender, gaudily dressed Mexican advanced to meet him, hand outstretched.

El Pardo!

The gunman backed his mount a few paces, then heeled it around. Still looking over his shoulder into the street, he failed to see the dim figure of a man standing in the shadows less than seventy feet away.

"Takin' another ride, Thompson?"

The gunman knew the voice. Swiveling his head, he said casually, "Howdy, Kerby."

The ex-lawman, six-gun in hand, stepped closer. "What's out in the street you don't like, Thompson?"

The gunman shrugged his shoulders, watching Kerby through narrowed eyes. He said calmly, "Don't know what you're talkin' about. Figured on takin' a little ride along the river this mornin'."

"You just rode in from the river," Kerby retorted, an ugly note in his voice. "The mud is hardly dry on the belly of your horse."

Thompson said, "All right, so I just rode in. What's the gun for?"

"They found Maxine this mornin', Thompson. Right where you left her. Dead!"

The expression on the gunman's face was intended to convey his surprise, but somehow it failed.

"Maxine dead? How?"

"You tell me!"

"You're loco, man, if you think I know anything about it!"

Kerby moved closer. "Get down!"

Thompson hesitated for a moment, weighing his chances.

"You heard him. Step down!"

The new voice came from the mouth of the alley, and the gunman didn't bother to turn his head. He swung from his saddle and held his hands shoulder high.

"Bowman, take the gun away from that fool before he kills someone!"

Kerby grated, "Keep out of this, Mace!"

Bowman moved from his position near the mouth of the alley, stopping a dozen feet to the right of the gunman.

"Drop your hands and toss your gun on the ground," he ordered. "Slow and easy."

Kerby's voice was deadly. "If you touch that gun, Thompson, I'll kill you!"

Dave Thompson stood motionless, looking from one to the other. He said at last, "What's it going to be, gents?"

Kerby's eyes never left the face of the gunman. "Mace, this coyote killed Maxine! I'm fixin' to plant a bullet in his yellow heart, gun or no gun!"

Bowman asked, "Why are you so sure he killed the girl, Jim?"

"Thompson went upstairs last night in the Maverick, and Maxine followed a few minutes behind him," the ex-lawman said. "Neither came down again. I waited in the saloon until an hour before dawn."

The gunman laughed disparagingly. "There's more than one way down from those rooms, mister! I talked with Maxine for a few minutes last night, then left by the outside stairs."

Kerby was about to make a savage retort, but Bowman held up his hand.

"Maybe Thompson killed the girl, Jim, but we'll never prove it in court," he said slowly. "Maxine was the only witness, and she won't be doin' any talkin'."

Kerby said roughly, "I wasn't thinkin' of a court, Mace! I'll start this coyote on his way to Boot Hill right now!"

"With a bullet?" Bowman asked. "That's too easy, Jim. Maybe I can't prove he killed the girl, but I've got enough right now to put him on the wrong end of a swingin' rope."

"I aim to see him crawlin' in the dust!"

"I won't stop you, if that's the way you want it," the sheriff said quietly. "I reckon Thompson deserves anything he gets. But think it over, son. A rope or a bullet?"

He pushed his hat to the back of his head, drawing his sleeve across his forehead.

"A rope, and you're in the clear," he pointed out. "A bullet, and maybe you've lost everything, even Mary Pearson."

Some of the tension seemed to seep from Kerby's body at the mention of the girl's name. He said finally, "What've you got on him, Mace?"

Bowman didn't answer immediately, turning instead to the gunman. "Drop your belt, Thompson, Pronto!"

Thompson complied without a word, his eyes riveted on the face of the lawman. Parting with the gun meant little; what worried him now was the sheriff's calm assurance that he had the evidence to hang him.

"You mean, what does Bowman *think* he has on me!" he jeered half-heartedly.

Bowman said curtly, "You're under arrest for the kidnappin' of *Señora* El Pardo and Marguerita Cardenas. In this part of the country, Thompson, kidnappin' is a hangin' offense!"

Thompson laughed, this time in sheer relief.

"You'll never pin anything like that on me!" he boasted. "This must be one of your jokes, Bowman."

"Sure, just a joke," the sheriff agreed. He stepped close to the gunman and grabbed him by the left arm just below the shoulder. Thompson winced visibly before he could steel himself as sudden pain shot through his arm.

Bowman said grimly, "That's about the way I had it figured!" His big hand ripped the gaudy shirt at the shoulder, stripping it down the gunman's arm. An ugly, red-edged gash was clearly visible on the white flesh of the arm.

He demanded roughly, "Who shot you?"

"No one shot me," Thompson denied quickly.

"Gashed myself on a nail in the livery stable a few days back."

"You're the gent who took a shot at me in front of the Maverick and hit Lucy Jensen!" the lawman said harshly. "Maybe I can't prove it, any more than I can prove you killed Maxine, but you'll hang all the same."

"You talk real big, Sheriff," Thompson said scornfully, "to a man without a gun!"

Bowman pointed to the ground at the gunman's feet. "There it is, Thompson. Pick it up if you feel lucky."

Thompson grinned at him. "Not this time, Sheriff. But my time will come, and when it does—"

He made a slashing motion across his throat with a finger. Farther along in the shadows of the stable, Jim Kerby sheathed his gun, feeling relief wash over him. He turned away, but Bowman was calling his name, and he faced the lawman.

"Mary will be mighty worried about you, Jim," Bowman was saying. "Reckon I'd see her right off if I was you!"

Kerby nodded and walked into the sunlight.

## *Ten*

At dusk, the weekly stage from Mission came to a squealing stop in front of the Border Hotel. It carried mail, but there were no passengers on board, and the bearded driver fully expected to begin the return trip early the following morning.

Mace Bowman was seated at his desk when Sandy Morgan brought in a handful of mail. Denver Rogers had not returned to Jurado, and Bowman thought it likely the young deputy had succeeded in sifting through El Pardo's encircling *vaqueros*. The sheriff shook his head, his forehead grooved with lines of worry. Even if Morgan had broken through the siege lines, he still faced a two-hundred-mile ride to the army post in the north, and El Pardo's deadline was little more than two days off.

Jurado was doomed.

Bowman leafed idly through the stack of mail, finding that all the letters except one contained routine flyers on wanted men. The exception was a letter from the United States marshal's office in Austin, written by Sam Carrigan, a law officer Bowman had known for many years.

"Dear Mace (the letter began),

"I've been looking forward to riding into Jurado one of these days and paying you a little surprise visit, but Uncle Sam has been keeping us mighty busy, so I guess I'll have to put it off for a while. But there is a matter you can help us with, and that is the purpose of this letter.

"Since your work does not usually touch upon such things, it's not likely you would know that we have been having considerable trouble in the last few months with the smuggling of drugs, particularly opium, from Mexico into this country. From a mere trickle at first, the flow of illegal opium has grown to such proportions that all border police have been alerted in an all-out effort to cut it off.

"Because of certain information which has come into my hands, I am almost certain that the smuggling is centered around Jurado. I can't check this out myself, but I am sending a deputy marshal into the area, and I know you will give him all the help he needs. With your long experience in border law enforcement, I am certain you will be of great use to him. He has orders to check into your office when he arrives, and the two of you can take it from there.

"I wish I could take this assignment myself, if for no other reason than that it would give me a chance to see an old friend, but it can't be worked out that way. So until I can thank you personally for your help, I remain faithfully yours,

Sam Carrigan"

Bowman read the letter over twice before he stuffed it back into the envelope and placed it carefully in a drawer of his desk.

Long before ten o'clock the next morning, every seat in Jurado's small courthouse was taken. Many, arriving too late to crowd into the room, gathered in small groups around the building, somber-faced and quiet. Inside the courtroom, the spectators seemed evenly divided between El Pardo's *vaqueros* and men and women from the town's meager population. Tension mounted swiftly, and those who spoke at all spoke in whispers; most said nothing at all.

Sandy Morgan was the first to arrive from the jail, with Dave Thompson striding arrogantly beside him.

Mace Bowman and Jason Ferriby, Dave's lawyer, came through the doorway together, but not from choice, and neither acknowledged the presence of the other. The lawyer took a seat near Dave Thompson, and Bowman slumped down at the front of the courtroom near the center aisle. Swiveling his head, he saw Juan El Pardo in the rear row of spectators, surrounded by bleak-faced *vaqueros*.

Judge Murphy came in from the small office directly behind the long table at the front of the room. None of the spectators rose to his feet, but Murphy seemed unaware of the breach of courtroom ethics. He was coatless and without a tie, concessions to the already stifling heat. He dropped into his chair and banged on the top surface of the table with a battered and worn gavel.

"This court is now in session!"

Murphy's eyes swept over the room, and he scowled when he saw the many *vaqueros* of Juan El Pardo. Bowman looked beyond the scowl and saw the fear, and knew Murphy would not put his own neck in a noose even to please Don Stillman.

Murphy said irritably, "The case before the court today is the people versus Dave Thompson, charged with kidnapping. How do you plead, Thompson?"

"Not guilty!"

"Do you wish a jury trial?"

"I'll let you be the judge, Murphy." Thompson grinned at his own joke.

Murphy glanced at Bowman. "Are you ready, Sheriff?"

The lawman nodded and signaled with a wave of his hand. Carlos, El Pardo's gate guard, rose from his seat near the back of the courtroom and made his way to the witness chair.

Judge Murphy intoned, "Do you swear to tell the truth, the whole truth and nothing but the truth, so help you God?"

"Yes."

Mace Bowman began the questioning of the witness without leaving his chair near the center aisle.

"Carlos, you were guardin' the main gates at the El Pardo hacienda last Tuesday mornin'?"

The *vaquero* nodded, his face flushed. "Yes."

"Were you alone?"

"At the gate, yes, but there were other *vaqueros* in the barns and stables, busy with the tasks assigned to them. *Señora* El Pardo and *Señorita* Cardenas were on the veranda of the hacienda."

"Did you see any strange riders that mornin' after Juan El Pardo left the hacienda?"

"Yes."

"How many?"

"Only one."

"Did you recognize that rider?"

"Not at the time, *señor,* but later I learned who he was."

"Do you see him in the courtroom?"

Carlos pointed with his finger. "It was *Señor* Thompson!"

The gunman, relaxed and confident, grinned across the room at the Mexican. Bowman saw the smile, and his face darkened.

He asked, "What did Thompson want?"

"He said he was carrying a message from you, and demanded to see *Señora* El Pardo."

Thompson said calmly, "That's a lie!"

Bowman ignored him. "Did you open the gates?"

"Only after *Señora* El Pardo ordered me to do so."

"At the time, you and the *señora* did not know the rider was Dave Thompson, the man who shot and killed Rafael Benavides?"

"No, or he would never have been allowed inside the gates!"

"Then what happened?"

"*Señor* Thompson spoke to the women on the veranda of the hacienda; then all three mounted and rode to the gate. The *señora* ordered me to open the gates, and I did so."

"Did Thompson speak to you as he left?"

"No, but he left a note which was signed with your name, threatening the lives of *Señora* El Pardo and *Señorita* Cardenas if Jurado was raided."

Bowman climbed to his feet and made his way to the witness stand. He fumbled in a pocket of his shirt and held out a soiled, heavily creased paper toward the Mexican.

"Is this the note Thompson left?"

The *vaquero* nodded, and Bowman tossed the paper on Judge Murphy's desk as he returned to his chair.

"You know my scrawl, Judge. That note was never written by me."

Murphy glanced at the paper.

"It doesn't appear to be your handwriting," he acknowledged. "But on the other hand, it doesn't prove Marshal Thompson wrote it, either."

Bowman turned back to the witness. "The last time you saw *Señora* El Pardo and *Señorita* Cardenas was in the company of Dave Thompson?"

"Yes."

"That's all, Carlos."

The *vaquero* rose to his feet, but Jason Ferriby called, "One moment, please!"

The lawyer left his seat and walked to a position in front of Judge Murphy. He said smoothly, "Your Honor, my client has never denied that he was at the El Pardo hacienda at the time in question, but he does deny that he was ever inside the gates, or that he had anything to do with the disappearance of the two women!"

Bowman said gruffly, "Don't make speeches, Ferriby. If you want to cross-examine the witness, get on with it."

Ferriby seemed about to make a retort, but changed his mind and turned to the Mexican. "Where was your master, Juan El Pardo, last Tuesday morning when the two women supposedly disappeared?"

"He was away from the hacienda on business," Carlos returned promptly.

"Just what was this business?"

Bowman stood up. "What El Pardo was doin' that mornin' has nothin' to do with this case, Your Honor. But if Ferriby thinks the court ought to know, El Pardo rode over to Virgil Storey's spread, rustled the cattle and burned the buildin's. This was one of the spreads Storey and Stillman stole from the Mexicans in the first place!"

A murmur of approval swept through the courtroom, and the lawyer flushed angrily. Bowman had cleverly taken the sting out his line of questioning, and he took another tack.

"You stated Dave Thompson claimed he was carrying a message from Sheriff Bowman. Did anyone else hear him say that?"

Carlos squirmed in his chair. "No."

"Did anyone else see you open the gates and let Dave Thompson into the courtyard, as you claim?"

"The other *vaqueros* were busy completing their tasks, as I have already said. No one saw me open the gates."

Ferriby was pleased. "Now you say that *Señora* El Pardo commanded you to open the gates and allow them to pass through. Was she forced to give that order by Marshal Thompson or anyone else?"

The *vaquero* was obviously confused by the question. "I do not understand."

"Let me put the question another way," Ferriby said smoothly. "Did Marshal Thompson hold a gun or a knife or any other weapon on the *señora* when she gave you the order to open the gate?"

"*Señor* Thompson had a gun."

"Was he carrying it in his hand, or was it holstered?"

"Holstered."

"Then the *señora* gave the order of her own accord?"

"*Señora* El Pardo feared for her life and for the life of *Señorita* Cardenas. That is the weapon *Señor* Thompson used to force her to open the gates."

Ferriby said, "Of course!" and laughed dryly. "Now we come to a part of your testimony which agrees with Dave Thompson's version of the affair. He admits that he rode away from the gates with the women, but only because they requested that he accompany them as far as the Jurado trail. Carlos, did you see a weapon in the hands of the marshal at any time?"

"No," Carlos was forced to admit.

"In other words, since you saw no weapon in the hands of the marshal, obviously he is telling the truth when he states that the women rode with him willingly?"

"No! They would not go willingly with such a jackal!"

Ferriby smiled at the outburst. "You call a man duly appointed marshal of Jurado a jackal?"

The *vaquero* said angrily, "He is that and worse!"

"In what direction did Marshal Thompson and the

women ride after they left the gates?"

"To the north."

"Would that be in the direction of the Jurado trail?"

"Yes."

"Marshal Thompson has maintained in a sworn statement that he rode with the women only as far as the Jurado trail. He has stated that he left them there to continue their journey to Jurado while he circled back to the river. Now think carefully, Carlos. Did you see the marshal do any differently from what he says he did?"

"The Jurado trail is many miles from the hacienda," Carlos said scornfully. "No one could observe *Señor* Thompson's actions from within the walls of the hacienda."

"Thank you, Carlos!" Ferriby said suavely. "That will be all."

The flustered and angry *vaquero* left the witness chair as the lawyer turned to Judge Murphy.

"Your Honor," he said persuasively, "if this is all the evidence Sheriff Bowman can bring against my client, I must demand that these ridiculous charges be dismissed! The witness is obviously biased; he dislikes the marshal even to the extent of referring to him as a jackal. He claims Thompson was inside the gates of the hacienda, but we have only his unsupported word as to the truth of that statement. He admits Marshal Thompson used no threats when he rode toward the Jurado trail—"

Bowman broke in. "Carlos said Thompson had no weapons in his hands. There's a difference."

"—And he has not disproved Thompson's claim that he left the two women on the Jurado trail," the lawyer continued as if he had not been interrupted. "I move at this time that the charges against the marshal be dismissed!"

Judge Murphy looked at Bowman. "Jason seems to have made a point, Sheriff. Do you have any other witnesses to help prove your case?"

Bowman, without speaking, climbed to his feet and moved toward a small anteroom on the right side of the courtroom. Dave Thompson was grinning confidently, and Jason Ferriby had a satisfied smile on his lips. Bowman reached the door of the small room and threw it open.

Standing just inside, surrounded by a dozen *vaqueros*, were *Señora* El Pardo and *Señorita* Cardenas!

Dave Thompson had the dazed look of a man who had just heard his death sentence pronounced, but he reacted with the savage cunning of a cornered rat. Wheeling, he drove his fist into the face of Sandy Morgan and leaped to his feet. Morgan made a futile grab for his arm, but the gunman eluded him, smashing the edge of his hand across the young deputy's neck and bringing his knee up into his face. Blood spurted, and Morgan fell backward across the bench as Thompson dove past him toward the small office behind the table.

The spectators were on their feet, milling and shouting, and the resulting confusion worked in favor of the fleeing gunman. Bowman, six-gun in hand, tried in vain to find an opening for a clear shot at the escaping prisoner, but the crowd, pushing and shoving, effectively blocked his view. Shouting for Morgan, he battled his way toward the door of the office, reaching it about the same time as the deputy.

Bowman kicked the door open and pushed into the room, but the precious moments they had lost fighting their way through the crowd had been enough; the room was empty. Bowman leaned far out the open window, but the gunman had made good his daring escape.

"Get a posse together, Sandy," Bowman ordered tersely. "Comb the town, but don't go too far out into the mesquite. If Thompson makes it that far, he'll cut you down one at a time and laugh while he's doin' it."

Returning to the now quiet courtroom, Bowman saw

Judge Murphy signaling for him to come to the table. Jason Ferriby, determined not to be left out, also hurried up.

"I guess you made your point, Sheriff," Murphy said as the big lawman ambled up. "Dave Thompson looked as if he were seeing ghosts when you opened that door."

"Maybe he thought he was," Bowman said grimly. "I stumbled across his hide-out the other night on my way in from the river. I took the women out of the cabin and put the torch to it. I reckon Thompson figured they went up in smoke with the shack."

Murphy looked at the lawyer. "You have anything to say, Jason?"

"What is there to say?" Ferriby countered. "The trial can't continue until Thompson is re-captured."

"Knowing what's in store for him if he is caught, I don't think he'll allow himself to be taken alive," Murphy said.

"The posse has orders to shoot on sight," Bowman said tersely. "I aim to do the same thing if I lay eyes on him."

"I must warn you, Sheriff, that Dave Thompson has not as yet been convicted of a crime," Ferriby said icily.

"He attacked a lawman and broke out of custody," Bowman retorted. "That makes him legal game for anyone who gets him in their gunsights, even under the kind of law Murphy hands out!"

The sheriff wheeled and started for the door, almost colliding with Manuel Hernandez, who had come up quietly behind him. He muttered a quick, "Sorry, Manuel," and tried to step around the blind man, but Hernandez held up his hand.

"*Señor* Bowman," he said contritely, "I am sorry my words put you in danger the other night."

The sheriff's keen eyes studied the blind man. "At the time I was mighty sorry myself, Manuel. Looked as if someone steered me into a deadfall."

Hernandez appeared stricken. "Surely you cannot suspect that I willingly sent you into an ambush?"

Bowman said evenly, "I might, if I could figure out a reason for you to want me dead.

"But we have been *amigos* for many years!"

"I know," the lawman returned curtly. "It's likely the only reason I didn't clap you in a cell!"

The *vaquero* hesitated for a moment, then said in a clear voice, "I have further information which may be of value to you, *Señor* Bowman. I wish to make a statement."

Judge Murphy growled, "This court is not in session, Hernandez. Make your statement in the sheriff's office."

"I will make it here!" the blind man said firmly. "*Señor* Bowman, I did not tell you all I knew about the attack upon the padre when you questioned me, because I was in fear of my life. I will tell you now."

Bowman asked bluntly, "Why?"

"Because a man, even a blind man, cannot live his life as a coward."

"All right, Manuel. Go ahead."

Judge Murphy rose to his feet behind the table. "This is a matter for you, Sheriff. I have other things to do."

Bowman snapped, "Sit down, Murphy!" and the judge reluctantly dropped back into his chair.

"Two days before the attack on *Señor* Benteen, I heard two men plotting to hire others to do the actual shooting," the blind man said. "I have heard their voices and footsteps many times, and I know them well."

"You should've come to me then," Bowman said roughly. "Who were they?"

Hernandez said instantly, "Don Stillman was one of them!"

"That much figures," Bowman agreed. "Will you testify to that in court?"

"Yes!"

"Who was the other hombre?"

"He was the leader," Hernandez replied in a low voice, "the one giving the orders."

A hush had fallen over the few spectators who had crowded to the front of the courtroom.

Bowman repeated impatiently, "Who was he?"

The Mexican raised his hand, and an unbelieving gasp swept through the room.

His finger pointed unerringly at Judge Murphy!

Bowman's six-gun was out and leveled at the raging judge, and he did not see the small, self-satisfied smile playing at the corners of the blind man's lips as he turned and made him way slowly up the aisle.

## Eleven

Juan El Pardo was back at his post on the veranda of
the Border Hotel. He had not approached Bowman
after the dramatic escape of Dave Thompson, nor had
any of his *vaqueros* taken part in the frenzied search
for the gunman. *Señora* El Pardo and *Señorita* Cardenas had been sent back to the hacienda under heavy
guard, and still others of El Pardo's band prowled the
streets of Jurado in ever-increasing numbers. The Mexican leader sat silent and alone on the veranda of the
hotel, his face bleak and foreboding.

After slamming the door of a cell behind the furious
Anson Murphy, Mace Bowman left the jail and headed
for the Maverick. He lifted his hand in a brief salute as
he passed the hotel, and El Pardo's slight nod was his
only response to the greeting. As Bowman was about to
turn into the cool interior of the saloon, he looked up

and saw Denver Rogers at the far end of the street. He turned and moved to the edge of the boardwalk, waiting patiently as the deputy reined in his mount and climbed stiffly from the saddle.

He called, "Howdy, Mace!"

The devastating effects of days on the open trail showed clearly on the deeply lined, weary face of the stocky deputy. Unshaven, his clothes thick with dust and the strains of the trail, Rogers looked more like a drifting saddle tramp than like an officer of the law.

Mace Bowman took the deputy by the arm, jerking his head in the direction of the Maverick.

"Hold the palaver, son, until we wash some of the cotton from your throat," he suggested.

Once inside the saloon, neither man spoke again until Denver had finished his second glass of cool, foaming beer and ordered a third.

"I've seen the time, in the last couple of days, when I might've given my right arm for a glass of this," he remarked, smacking his lips.

Bowman observed, "It's not likely you reached the fort and rode back here in the time you've been gone."

The deputy shook his head. "I rode across the river, like you said, then turned east. No one tried to stop me, so I reckon I was either lucky or El Pardo didn't figure on anyone tryin' to slip out the back door. I cut back across the river about twenty miles east of here and headed for the fort."

He drank deeply of the cool liquid in his glass.

"Ran across Colonel Elkton and about two hundred of his horse soldiers," he continued. "Happened they were out on field manuevers, or so the colonel said. They're on their way here now, less than a day behind me."

He emptied his glass and signaled the bartender. "I rode in ahead, figurin' you might want a chance to talk El Pardo out of the border country. He's a goner for sure if he tries to brace Elkton and his soldiers."

Bowman briefly recounted the happenings in the town while the deputy was out on the trail.

"Neither Stillman or Murphy will talk," he concluded. "But I figure we have enough on them even without Santos and Payne."

"What happens now?"

"Depends a lot on what Colonel Elkton does when he gets here," the sheriff replied. "If he puts Jurado under martial law, the army can handle it. Otherwise we'll just have to wait for a new judge to be appointed. Either way, the Mexicans are bound to get their land back."

"How about El Pardo?"

"It's likely the El Pardo family will get their land back," Bowman replied. "As for Juan, it depends a lot on whether or not he keeps his promise to raze the town, and if he elects to fight when the army gets here. Anyway, he'll have to face trial for what happened to John Navarre and Ben Gates."

"I reckon Dave Thompson is flaggin' the dust away from here as fast as he can push his bronc," the deputy commented.

Bowman shook his head. "It's my guess he's still in the border country, Denver. He'll stay close to Jurado as long as he figures he has a chance to finish what he started, so maybe we'll put him under a hangin' tree yet!"

Jim Kerby drifted in as Bowman moved toward the door. For a moment it appeared that Kerby would stop the lawman; then he stepped aside and nodded slightly as Bowman passed. Outside, Manuel Hernandez greeted him as he always did, and the lawman paused briefly by his side. Bowman, too, seemed about to open a conversation; then he changed his mind and headed for the Border Hotel. Juan El Pardo was still in his chair on the veranda, near the door of the hotel, and Bowman toed up a chair beside him.

"We'll get Thompson," he said grimly. "Depend on it, Juan."

The Mexican nodded politely but said nothing.

"Murphy and Stillman are in cells," Bowman continued. "The rest of their bunch are under guard in their hotel rooms."

He removed his hat and wiped the sweat from his forehead with the sleeve of his shirt. "You and your people will have your lands once again, without fightin' or other violence."

Juan El Pardo stirred restlessly in his chair. "And what will happen to Juan El Pardo?"

"That depends on what happened to John Navarre and Ben Gates," Bowman said frankly. "If they've been harmed, you'll have to stand trial."

"Before another man like Anson Murphy?" El Pardo asked bitterly.

"The next judge will be a man interested only in justice," Bowman replied soberly. "I promise you that, Juan."

The Mexican was again silent, and Bowman said, "The soldiers will be here before mornin', *amigo*."

El Pardo looked deep into his eyes and saw the truth of his words. "And you sent for them, my friend?"

"I sent Rogers for them," Bowman acknowledged.

"He broke through your *vaqueros* and met the soldiers a day's ride from here. If you try to brace them, *amigo*, they'll drive you into the river."

"I have made certain promises to my people," El Pardo said thoughtfully.

"Your promises will be kept when their lands are returned to them. There is no reason for bloodshed."

"I have told them I will burn Jurado unless Stillman and his jackals are placed in my hands."

"It was a foolish promise!" Bowman said sharply, "made in anger and without thought!"

"It is a matter of honor!"

"If your honor brings a hundred graves to Jurado, then you will fill the first one!" Bowman warned grimly. "You will never live to see the torch put to the town!"

He added, his eyes bleak, "And that threat is a matter of honor with me, Juan."

El Pardo was silent for some time; then he said in an even voice, "What is it you would have of me?"

"Your promise not to turn your *vaqueros* loose in Jurado," Bowman replied promptly. "If you fear standin' trial, then ride below the border with your *vaqueros*, where you will be out of reach of the soldiers."

El Pardo considered. "I will give you my answer before dawn."

The darkness over the border town was heavy, for dusk was past and the moon had not yet risen. Jim Kerby moved through the alley with slow, careful steps, only occasionally catching a glimpse of the man he was following. A small barn loomed ahead of his quarry, and the man paused, as if listening for any possible pursuers. Then he disappeared from the ex-lawman's sight, and a moment later Kerby heard the squeaking of rusty hinges.

He waited for a further sound, and when none came, he made his way cautiously to the side of the barn, to a small, dust-covered window. Inside the stable a small candle had been lighted, and Kerby could see a vague, shadowy figure kneeling in the center of the room. The man was clearing a space on the straw-littered floor with his bare hands, but the light was too dim and the window too grimy for Jim to see who it was. The stranger seemed to be searching for something, and a moment later Kerby heard him give a grunt of satisfaction as he reached down and swung a trap door wide.

Kerby shifted his feet to get a better view, and a can rattled across the ground. Instantly the light inside the stable blinked out and he heard the slamming of the trap door. Cursing softly under his breath, he raced around the corner of the building toward the door the stranger had used in entering the stable. The hinges howled as he threw it wide, but even as he stepped inside he heard the slamming of a door at the rear of the building and knew it would be useless to try to follow the stranger in the darkness.

He struck a match and found the candle stub the intruder had left behind him. In the flickering light he knelt beside the trap door and raised it slowly, revealing a scooped-out hole not more than two feet square. The cavity beneath the floor was more than half filled with round, flat tins and a number of small, bulky cloth bags. Kerby was reaching for one of the tins when a voice spoke near the open door.

"Climb back on your feet, Jim," Mace Bowman ordered curtly, "and keeep your hands over your head."

Bowman was standing just inside the door, a leveled six-gun in his hand. Kerby lifted himself to his feet, his hands held shoulder high, and waited for the lawman to speak. Bowman came forward slowly, motioned Kerby back from the trap door and glanced down at the cache. He whistled softly between his teeth.

"I don't know much about this sort of thing," he said thoughtfully. "But I hear they ship opium in tins like that."

Kerby said calmly, "It *is* opium!"

Bowman's eyes were puzzled as he studied the ex-lawman. "Maybe you can tell me what's in those bags?"

"Gold coins, most likely."

Bowman shook his head. "Never figured you for a play like this, Jim. Carrigan won't believe you were tied up with the smugglin', either."

Kerby grinned. "That stuff's not mine, Mace."

"No? I reckon you just happened to stumble across this cache." Bowman's voice was skeptical.

"I followed someone here. I made a little too much noise and scared him away."

"This is Anson Murphy's stable, but it's a cinch you didn't follow him here. He's still locked up nice and tight in that cell of mine."

"I don't know who it was, Mace. It was too dark in the alley to recognize him, and the window was too dirty to get a good look at him. Besides, his back was toward me most of the time."

"Your story is mighty thin, Jim. Why would *you* follow anyone anywhere?"

"Maybe it was just curiosity, Mace. I saw this gent turn down the alley and I followed him. It's as simple as that."

"Maybe to you, but not to me. Drop your gun on the floor, Jim. Careful!"

Kerby gingerly removed his six-gun from its holster and let it drop to the floor. "You've got this all wrong, Mace."

"If I have, someone else will have to tell me. Now head for the door."

"Where are we goin'?"

"To the jail. I figure on you keepin' Stillman and Murphy company for a spell."

"Look, Mace, I can clear this up right now!"

His fingers fumbled with his belt and he flipped a shining object in the air toward the sheriff. Bowman caught it in his left hand and glanced at it quickly, cautioning Kerby to stay back with a wave of his gun. He exclaimed, "Well, I'll be—!"

"I thought you might be." Kerby grinned.

Bowman holstered his gun and grinned ruefully. "So you're the U.S. deputy marshal that Sam Carrigan wrote me about!"

"Reckon I am."

"Why didn't you tell me who you were when you rode into town?"

Kerby looked uncomfortable. "It's this way, Mace. I didn't trust anyone, not even you. You've been in the border country a long time, and the way I figured it, who would be in a better position to pull a stunt like this?"

"Likely to figure the same way myself, in your shoes," Bowman grunted.

Kerby stooped and picked up his gun, sliding it back into his holster. "But I've been watchin' you mighty close, Mace, and I couldn't figure you for a part in this."

"What about all that stuff in the paper?" Bowman asked. "That a put-up job?"

"No," Kerby replied reluctantly. "I had to shoot Billy Janus, but only after he planted a bulletin in my arm. He was a real bad actor, just like his two brothers who were in on the robbery with him. The editor of the Abilene paper never saw eye to eye with me, and he really gave me the works when he had the chance."

"The story got you a job with Don Stillman."

"Stillman's not our man. For a while I figured it might be you; then this hombre I followed tonight turned up."

"Maybe he works for Anson Murphy."

"Maybe, but I don't figure he's loco enough to hide the stuff in his own stable."

Kerby knelt by the open trap door and picked up one of the cloth bags. He pulled the drawstring loose and upended it on the floor.

"Gold coins!" Bowman exclaimed. "Jim, there must be fifty or sixty thousands dollars in those bags!" He released a deep breath. "Let's tote this stuff over to the jail, Jim, before we get tempted. Maybe Murphy and Stillman will be ready to talk when we shove this under their noses!"

But the two lawmen did not find Don Stillman in his cell when they returned to the jail. He was seated at a table in a small, run-down shack beside the river, and across from him, casually studying the land specu-lator, was Dave Thompson.

Thompson said bluntly, "Don't see where you have much choice in the matter, Don."

The candle stub, firmly embedded in a mound of its own drippings in the center of the table, flickered and smoked as the freshening wind found its way through the cracks and crevices in the ancient walls. Stillman returned the steady gaze of the gunman.

"I'm not thinking of choices," he said thoughtfully. "I'm only wondering what good it will do if I sign everything I'm supposed to own over to you."

With Mace Bowman and every deputy in Jurado

looking for him, the gunman had slipped back into town at dusk and broken Don Stillman out of jail.

Don now said, "They'll hang you if you show your face in Jurado, Dave; now or in a hundred years!"

Thompson grinned across the table.

"I'll make it," he boasted confidently. "Sooner or later the army is bound to take care of El Pardo and his *vaqueros*. That'll leave Bowman and maybe Kerby. Those two hombres live and die the same as the rest of us, Don. I aim to give them a little nudge toward Boot Hill!"

Stillman, accustomed to a certain amount of savage ruthlessness, nevertheless shuddered as he listened to the cold voice of the gunman.

"You've done a lot of killing, Dave," he said slowly. "Some of it doesn't make much sense. Take the girl, Maxine."

"No one killed Maxine," Thompson retorted irritably. "She was doin' a little drinkin' that night, and she tripped on a rug near the window and fell out. I was in the room, and I know."

Knowing the boastful nature of the gunman, Stillman was sure he was speaking the truth. "At first we blamed El Pardo for Nick Valdes, but now I think it was you."

"He served his purpose," Thompson said curtly.

"And El Pardo was handy to take the blame."

"You want to be a big man along the border," the land speculator mused. "And you figure murder and violence will make you one. I guess I thought that way once, too, and now I'm one step ahead of a hanging rope."

"You were stupid!" the gunman said viciously. "You didn't have the sand to do your own dirty work, and that gave others a hold over you. I won't make the same mistake!"

He tossed a folded piece of paper across the table. "Sign it, Don."

Stillman moved his heavy shoulders in resignation. "I'll sign, Dave, but it won't meant a thing. I don't own a piece of property anywhere along the border!"

The chair Thompson was sitting in crashed to the floor as he leaped to his feet and crouched over the table.

He snarled, "What are you tryin' to put over on me?"

"Nothing, Dave. I'm only telling you I don't own *any* property in the border country and never have!"

Thompson controlled his rising anger with difficulty. "Who owns the saloons and store in Jurado and the ranches if you don't?"

"Anson Murphy."

"Murphy! I thought—"

"You thought he was working for me, but it's the other way around. Murphy devised the plan to take over the land of the Mexicans even before we came to Jurado. He sent me ahead to lay the groundwork, and when he came he stayed in the background."

Thompson slid his six-gun from its holster. "You tricked me!"

"No, Dave. You believed what everyone else believed because you wanted to."

Stillman read his sentence in the cruel eyes of the gunman, but he seemed drained of all emotion, and no words of pleading came from his lips.

"I knew you had it planned this way, Dave, even if I could have turned everything over to you," he said quietly. "I was certain of it from the moment you turned the key in the lock of my cell. But a man can't run forever, and a bullet looks better to me than a rope."

"Glad you feel that way about it, Don," Thompson said sarcastically, his finger beginning to squeeze the trigger. Then he laughed coarsely and dropped the gun back into its holster.

"I'm not goin' to shoot you, Don." He grinned.

"After I leave, you're free to walk out that door!"

"So you can shoot me from somewhere out there in the darkness?"

Thompson was still grinning. "Why waste a bullet on you, Don? It's too quick, and it's what you want. So you're tired of running? Mister, with both the law and El Pardo on your trail, you'll run until you drop!"

He was still grinning when he walked slowly from the room.

## Twelve

The fire was discovered by a drunk crawling on his hands and knees along a debris-strewn alley at the west end of the town. Perched unsteadily on his hands and knees, the drunk watched in fascination as it blazed higher and closer. When the flames began to scorch his clothing, he backed away, succeeded in staggering to his feet and lurching into the street. But for Jurado, his warning shouts came too late.

Denver Rogers, one of several deputies patroling the town after the daring escape of Don Stillman, saw the fire and heard the drunk at the same time. Wheeling, he dashed for the sheriff's office, his shouts spreading the dread alarm.

Fire!

Bowman met him at the door, saw the reason for his excitement over his shoulder and said harshly, "El

Pardo!"

"Not El Pardo, my friend," the slim Mexican said swiftly, stepping from the shadows to the right of the door. "Neither El Pardo nor any of his *vaqueros* held the torch which started this fire!"

Bowman said curtly, "Then get your *vaqueros* and give us a hand, or stand out of the way!"

Somewhere near the center of town the fire triangle was clanging out its dread message, and the narrow street began filling with excited men and women, milling and shoving in confusion. Buildings on both sides of the street at the west end of town were shooting long streamers of smoke and burning debris into the air, and the fire began advancing toward the center of Jurado with startling speed. The sky caught the reflection of the blaze and hurled it back at the town, bathing it in a flickering, dancing red glow of destruction.

Jim Kerby came around the corner of the jail, six-gun in hand.

"Dave Thompson is in town!" he said tersely. "Caught a glimpse of him in the alley near the Mercantile, but I couldn't get a clean shot at him."

The sheriff said grimly, "He had a hand in this, then," and moved into the center of the street. Long bucket lines had already formed at several wells, but the lawman knew the fire would never be contained with the few drops of water the sweating men could provide. The combined efforts of El Pardo's *vaqueros* working side by side with the grim-faced inhabitants of the town seemed puny in the face of the roaring wall of flame.

Bowman called, "Denver!" and when the deputy appeared, ordered, "Take some help over to the Mercantile and pick up some blasting powder, pronto! We'll blow the buildings on both sides of the street just ahead of the fire. It's our only chance."

He moved down the center of the street, now crowded with men, women and children of all ages, and selected the buildings in which to use the blasting powder.

"Get back!" he shouted angrily as the crowd surged against him. "Get back and give us room!"

The restless crowd quickly opened a path when they saw Denver Rogers and another deputy trotting up with kegs of blasting powder on their shoulders. Juan El Pardo pushed his way to the side of the lawman, followed by Carlos and several other *vaqueros*.

"Carlos has handled blasting powder many times," he told Bowman. "He will place the charges for you."

"All right," Bowman assented instantly. "We'll use

the powder in Benteen's old church on the north side of the street. On the south side, the livery stable should do the trick."

Carlos and two of El Pardo's *vaqueros*, working against time and in the face of scorching heat, quickly had the powder charges in place and fuses attached. At a signal from Bowman, Carlos touched a burning torch to the ends of the fuses, and a moment later the doomed buildings disintegrated in a mighty display of smoke and flame.

Denver Rogers came up to where Mace Bowman stood watching the effects of the blasts.

"It's no good, Mace," he said worriedly. "The wind is too strong."

The sheriff saw that Rogers was right. Already the surging flames had leaped the gaps created by the blasting powder, and the drought-parched buildings on both sides of the street were burning fiercely. It seemed nothing more could be done to save the town.

"Round up all the able-bodied men you can find," Bowman ordered tonelessly. "Have them get the women and children out to the east edge of town as fast as they can. We haven't much time left."

Turning away, he saw Doc Jarrett and Juan El Pardo carry the blanket-wrapped form of Lucy Jensen from the doctor's house and place her gently in the bed of a wagon. The old doctor waved his hand as he climbed to the seat of the wagon, and Bowman knew that Lucy was all right. He looked around for Jim Kerby, but the lawman had disappeared. The street was clearing rapidly as the townspeople gathered up the few articles they could save from their homes and dashed for the east end of Jurado and safety.

The fire closed in, and Bowman backed down the street. He found the Border Hotel already in flames and the west wall of the Maverick beginning to char. Manuel Hernandez was still seated in his chair in front of the saloon, his calm face showing none of the mounting hysteria evident in the voices of the fleeing inhabitants.

Mace stopped briefly in front of the blind *vaquero*. He ordered tersely, "Get out of this while you can!" and wheeled toward the entrance to the Maverick. In all probability, the sudden move saved his life. Orange flame lanced out from the corner of the saloon, and he felt the shock of a bullet as it cut a heavy furrow through the flesh of his upper left arm. Spinning on his heel, he dropped into the dust of the street and rolled toward the edge of the boardwalk. Twice more the hidden gun blasted out its savage message of death, but the bullets pounded into the dust wide of their target.

It began to rain. At first there were only scattered drops of moisture fighting their way through the heavy pall of smoke overhead, then more and bigger drops of water until the rain came down in a hissing roar upon the burning town. The thirsty dust of the street, parched and powdered for almost four months, drank deeply of the moisture until, sated, it began to turn into a muddy quagmire.

Bowman, from behind the meager shelter of a half-burned wagon, saw Dave Thompson dart toward the open door of the Maverick, smoking six-gun in hand. He drew his own weapon and fired in the same smooth motion, but the gunman had already disappeared into the darkened interior of the saloon, and the bullet thudded harmlessly into the frame of the door. Almost before the sound of the shot had faded away, the lawman was on his feet and racing for the front of the saloon. Risking a quick glance through an open window, he saw that the west wall of the Maverick was already in flames and the big room was rapidly filling with drifting eddying streamers of smoke. Dropping away from the window, he circled the corner of the building and disappeared into the darkness of the alley.

Across the street Jim Kerby ran from the mouth of

the alley where he had witnessed the explosive ex-
change of shots. As Bowman turned the corner of the
building, Kerby raced across the street toward the
front entrance of the saloon and slipped inside, picking
his way cautiously to the center of the room. The heat
from the blazing west wall beat against him and he
was forced back toward the entrance.

"Wait!"

Kerby stopped short in his tracks, instantly recognizing the owner of the voice. He twisted his head
slowly, and the smoke-obscured figure of Dave Thompson came into his view. The gunman's teeth showed in
a wolfish grin as he leaned against the railing of the
balcony, leveled six-gun in his hand.

"I've been waitin' for the sheriff to show his face,
Kerby, but you'll do!" he said evilly. "The shoe's on
the other foot this time!"

Standing helplessly in the midst of the heat and
smoke below the balcony, Kerby knew he could not
hope to draw and shoot before the gunman sent a bullet crashing into his back. But since there was no other
choice left open to him, his hand flashed with stunning
speed to his holstered gun. Thompson's weapon roared,
and Kerby was driven forward by the shock of the
bullet pounding high into the muscles of his back. He

staggered drunkenly, losing his gun as he fought for balance, and fell face down on the sawdust-littered floor.

Slowly and painfully he rolled to his side, his hand reaching out for the gun scant inches from the tips of his fingers. From his vantage point on the balcony, Thompson triggered his weapon again, and the bullet slit the skin just over Kerby's right ear. Eyes blurring, total darkness crowding his brain, he watched helplessly as the misty figure of the gunman brought his gun to bear for a finishing shot.

"Over here, Thompson!"

Mace Bowman, standing a dozen feet to the left and rear of the renegade gunman, might have killed him without warning, but some deep-rooted sense of fairness stayed his finger, and the split-second delay gave Thompson his chance. Swinging his gun across his body, he fired a quick shot under his left armpit. The bullet, a little wide, broke Bowman's right wrist, driving the gun from his fingers.

The shock spun Bowman against the wall. But, recovering quickly, he dropped to one knee and scooped up the six-gun with his left hand, firing in the same motion. The bullet barely scraped the point of Thompson's shoulder, but it was enough to send his second

shot high over the lawman's head. On the floor below
the balcony, Jim Kerby's fingers closed painfully over
the butt of his gun, and it was his bullet which sent
the weapon spinning from the gunman's hand before
he could trigger another shot.

Bowman braced his heels against the wall and dove
headlong for the gunman, smashing him back against
the flimsy railing of the balcony. Below them smoke
and flames leaped up from the burning wall and floor.

The driving force of Bowman's rush splintered the
railing behind the gunman. Kerby, flat on his back on
the floor below, heard Thompson scream in terror and
watched with dimming eyes as the gunman fought for
balance, almost succeeded, then fell backward into the
pit of flames beneath the balcony. Bowman, unable to
check his rush, slipped over the edge of the balcony.
His right arm useless, the lawman made a frantic grab
for the edge of the flooring with his left hand and
momentarily arrested his fall.

Kerby tried to call out, but the words were scarcely
more than a mutter. Darkness dimmed his eyes and he
felt himself slipping into a velvety blackness devoid
of pain. A path cleared for an instant through the
swirling smoke, and he saw Mace Bowman's fingers
slowly slipping from their grip on the edge of the bal-

cony. He dimly heard someone in the distance calling his name as his eyes closed and his head dropped to the floor.

Bowman, desperately swinging his body as his fingers slipped from the edge of the balcony, struck the floor with a jarring thud just clear of the flames. He staggered drunkenly to his feet just as Juan El Pardo raced to his side, and together they pulled the unconscious gunman from the edge of the fire. His shirt was smoldering, and Bowman ripped the garment from his shoulders. Thompson had missed the seething pit of flames by a few inches, and his breathing was shallow but even.

"Hit his head when he fell from the balcony," Bowman guessed. "He'll live to hear a judge send him to the scaffold!"

El Pardo's *vaqueros* began crowding into the saloon, and the Mexican leader said, "I have a wagon outside, Mace," as the lawman dropped to his knees beside Jim Kerby. Bowman was grinning as he climbed back to his feet.

"Lost a little blood, but he'll be all right," he said. "Jim's too tough a lawman to let a couple of pieces of lead bother him much."

The *vaqueros* carried Kerby and the still unconscious gunman to the waiting wagon and, with El Pardo shouting orders, headed for the east end of town and Doc Jarrett. When Bowman reached the street he found the rain still coming down in torrents, and the street a sea of rutted mud. Manuel Hernandez still sat in his chair, seemingly oblivious to the drenching rain.

"The heavens have done what man could not," he said calmly as Bowman stopped near him. "The fires are almost out."

The lawman, still holding the six-gun in his left hand, was silent.

After a moment the Mexican continued, "A new town will rise on the ashes of the old; a better town, although I may not be here to see it."

Bowman still remained silent, his eyes watching the sputtering, dying flames as the rain drove against them.

Hernandez asked quietly, "How long have you known, *amigo?*"

"Not long," Bowman returned soberly. "When I stepped from the saloon just now and saw you sittin' in your chair, I remembered something."

"About the night Lucy Jensen was shot?"

"Yes. Someone called out, 'There's blood all over the front of her dress.' "

"I remember," the *vaquero* said in a low voice.

"How could a blind man, in a chair more than ten feet away, know that there was blood all over the front of Lucy's dress?"

"It was a slip I regretted instantly, my friend. I knew the time would come when you would remember whose voice it was that called out that night."

"Is that why you had an ambush set up for me at the river?"

"Santos and Payne worked for me as well as for Don Stillman," Hernandez returned. "I merely told them that you would ride to their cabin that night, and to be prepared for you."

"Why were you willing to testify against Murphy and Stillman?"

"Because they were the ones who stole the lands of my people and hired Santos and Payne to shoot the padre," the Mexican returned evenly. "I wanted peace and quiet to return to the border country."

"Because you knew if the soldiers came, your own apple cart might be upset?"

Hernandez shrugged but said nothing, and Bowman asked, "How long has it been since you regained your sight, Manuel?"

"A few months before my wife died last year. It was gradual at first, only blurs and shadows, but at last I could see as well as any man."

"Then you turned to smugglin' drugs. Why?"

The Mexican hesitated, and Bowman said, "It had to be you, *amigo*. When it came to me that you were responsible for the ambush at the river, I knew you wouldn't try to have me shot just because I might find out some day that you weren't blind. You weren't stealing the lands of your own people, and that left only the smugglin'. But why?"

"Why?" Hernandez repeated in a voice without emotion. "Why does a man do anything, my friend? For power, perhaps, or gold, or to erase a little of the filth and loneliness of the border country."

"The border country is the same to all of us," the sheriff returned gently. "It treats us all alike."

"Graves have been filled, tears shed," Hernandez said in a low voice. "On whose shoulders the blame must fall is of little concern to those whose eyes and lips have been sealed forever."

"It's my concern, *amigo*."

"It is ended, *Señor* Bowman. Would it not be best to leave it that way?"

"The law does not forgive or forget," Bowman said tersely. "The price must be paid."

He thumbed back the hammer of his six-gun, his

eyes on the stolid face of the *vaquero*. Hernandez turned at the sound.

"A bullet would be the easiest way, *Señor* Bowman."

"It would be the easiest," the lawman agreed.

"It would be hard to kill an old friend?"

"It would be hard."

Hernandez rose from his chair. "I must go, *Señor* Bowman. I leave Jurado behind me forever."

Bowman shook his head, the rain splattering from the brim of his hat. "You must come with me, *amigo*."

*"Vaya con dios, Señor* Bowman!"

Bowman brought up his gun but watched in silence as the Mexican started across the muddy street. A team drawing a wagon loaded with household furnishings raced toward him from the west end of town, and Hernandez stopped in the center of the street to allow it to pass. The horses were almost abreast of him when the blasting powder in the storeroom of the Mercantile, ignited by a stray ember, let loose with an earth-shaking roar. The team, wild-eyed with fright, veered sharply, and Manuel Hernandez, seemingly rooted to the spot where he stood, made no effort to escape their slashing hooves.

With the dawn came the end of the torrential rain.

Half of Jurado was a smoldering ruin, and the other half was crowded with those who had lost both homes and furnishings. Mace Bowman stood silently at the edge of the boardwalk as Juan El Pardo rode toward him down the muddy street at the head of his *vaqueros*. The slender Mexican nodded a greeting as he reined his mount to a stop near the lawman.

"There is nothing to hold us longer in Jurado," he said somberly. "I take my *vaqueros* back to the hacienda."

"I reckon I owe you a heap of thanks, Juan," Bowman replied.

"Perhaps I owe you more, my friend," the Mexican said gravely. "You have taught me that honor comes to a man in many ways." El Pardo started away, calling over his shoulder, "Send your deputies to my hacienda, *amigo*. John Navarre and Ben Gates are there, safely locked in a storeroom. When the new judge arrives, he will want to question them!"

Bowman grinned as he watched El Pardo and his *vaqueros* ride out of Jurado. Peace had come at last to the border country! Let the soldiers come; they could turn their hands from war to the task of rebuilding Jurado!

Across the street he saw Jim Kerby and Mary Pearson deep in conversation with Jack Benteen. Bowman thought idly: The padre is looking for marrying business, and by the looks of things, he's found it!

He turned in at the little white house where he knew Lucy Jensen would be waiting for him.